PENGUIN BOOKS

TALKING TO THE DEAD

'Dunmore is, without doubt, one of the most promising young writers around, combining a dazzling perceptiveness about the darker aspects of the human psyche with a heart-stoppingly compelling style' – *Cosmopolitan*

'As beautifully written and as psychologically gripping as her award-winning *A Spell of Winter*' – Christina Koning in *The Times*

'In her delicate, sensual prose, full of the scents and tastes of summer, Dunmore creates a poisoned idyll ... With exquisite finesse she anatomizes the deadly complicity between Nina and Isabel – their bond of love and jealousy and intimacy and betrayal, almost too tightly knotted to unravel' – Jane Shilling in the *Sunday Telegraph*

'Dunmore is a poet, and it shows here in her marvellously exact eye for the telling detail, her relish of landscape, her wonderful capacity for sensual evocation of nature' – Michèle Roberts in the *Independent on Sunday*

'Seething with guilt, erotic tension and unvoiced accusations, this compelling novel is about the danger of things left unsaid ... Dunmore paces the story to perfection, her flair for unusual imagery shining through the prose' – Gillian Fairchild in *Good Housekeeping*

'Electrifying' – Val Hennessy in the *Daily Mail*

ABOUT THE AUTHOR

Helen Dunmore is a novelist, short-story writer and poet. Her books include *Zennor in Darkness*, awarded the McKitterick Prize in 1994, *Burning Bright*, *A Spell of Winter*, winner of the 1996 Orange Prize for Fiction, *Talking to the Dead* and *Love of Fat Men*. All of these titles are published in Penguin. Her most recent novel, *Your Blue-Eyed Boy*, is published by Viking and forthcoming in Penguin. Her poetry collections include *The Sea Skater*, winner of the Poetry Society's Alice Hunt Bartlett Award, *The Raw Garden*, a Poetry Book Society Choice, and *Secrets*, winner of the 1995 Signal Poetry Award. A selection of her poems can be found in *Penguin Modern Poets 12*.

Helen Dunmore was born in Yorkshire and now lives in Bristol with her husband and children.

HELEN DUNMORE

Talking to the Dead

PENGUIN BOOKS

PENGUIN BOOKS

Published by the Penguin Group
Penguin Books Ltd, 27 Wrights Lane, London W8 5TZ, England
Penguin Putnam Inc., 375 Hudson Street, New York, New York 10014, USA
Penguin Books Australia Ltd, Ringwood, Victoria, Australia
Penguin Books Canada Ltd, 10 Alcorn Avenue, Toronto, Ontario, Canada M4V 3B2
Penguin Books (NZ) Ltd, Private Bag 102902, NSMC, Auckland, New Zealand

Penguin Books Ltd, Registered Offices: Harmondsworth, Middlesex, England

First published by Viking 1996
Published in Penguin Books 1997
10

Grateful acknowledgement is made to Faber and Faber for permission to print the
extract from 'Autiobiography' published in *Collected Poems* by Louis MacNiece

Printed in England by Clays Ltd, St Ives plc

Chapter One

The new graves lie full in the sun, beyond the shadow of the church and the yew tree. Two of them are covered in plastic-wrapped flowers and raw earth. These graves won't have stones for a while yet, because they must wait for the earth to settle.

There are a lot of things you need to know when someone dies, and you have to learn in a hurry, from people who are paid to teach you. They come up with hushed, serious faces and ask questions, and then they nudge you into finding the right answers. It's no good saying nothing, because they only keep on waiting. It's their job. *Have you considered the twenty-third psalm? Had the deceased a favourite hymn? Was there any connection with the church?* I knew what they meant by that. Were they going to have to write down a prompt card for the vicar, covered with useful, acceptable facts?

And how many will be coming back to the house? There'll be a limousine for immediate family, of course, but perhaps other cars will be required in view of the rather remote situation. There were two of them standing there, noting down the requirements. One glanced at the other, and they gleamed with satisfaction at phrasing it all so well. But they were much too professional to smile. They sounded like estate agents who were selling us our own lives.

And then the food. After a funeral you have to eat, to prove you're still alive. There are foods which are suitable, and foods which are not. The suitable ones turn out to be ham, or cold chicken. Quiche is very popular, and Australian wines. The unsuitable ones would be anything which required last-minute attention from drunk or weeping people. I was hungry myself. I ate the chicken sandwiches, and drank the wine.

I can remember every word that was said. I can remember

staring at a big glazed ham, its rind scored into squares and glistening with syrup. I thought of how it would be sliced and fed to us after your burial. Someone was asking me if I would like fresh pineapple to garnish the ham, or tinned.

'Will you want the coffin open, or closed?'

'Some people,' one of them whispered, 'some people find it a great comfort actually to have *seen*. Not to have to *imagine*. It can be a great comfort.'

'A great comfort,' I say aloud now, taking the words out like stones from my pocket, tossing them into the quiet air.

It's beautiful here, where you are. Tall brick and flint walls enclose the churchyard, but we're high up, and beyond the walls I can look out to the blue line of the Weald. The air moves freely. It's hot and dry and the earth smells like a body stretched out to bake in the sun. Bees have swarmed on the other side of the church. I went round just now, and saw them hanging there in a dark cluster under the roof. Stray bees zinged through the air towards the swarm, and their sound was dangerous, like water in a kettle which has nearly boiled dry. I came away lightly, scarcely breathing.

You are out in the sun, away from the yew tree. I remember once we were talking about why yew trees were planted in churchyards, and I told you that they were supposed to have powers to keep off evil spirits. You said that there was a good practical reason too. Farmers wouldn't let their animals graze in any enclosure where there was a yew tree, so the graves were respected.

Your stone is firm. I know exactly how much it cost, and how many letters there are in the inscription. There is just your full name, the name you've kept since childhood. You didn't want to change it when you married. Under your name are the dates of your birth and your death. No message, no reflection on your life. No clues at all. The only thing which might make anyone stop is the shortness of the time between the first date and the last. Someone might count up how long you'd lived, and wonder, and start to make up a story for you out of nothing.

People idling through graveyards always stop by the graves of the young. Hundreds of miles from here there's another grave with the same surname on it as yours, a tiny grave in a steep cemetery above the sea. There's a path through the cemetery which tourists use as a short cut down to the beach. They stop, read the inscription, the name and dates, and the two lines of poetry. Often there's a jamjar of flowers left on the grave. If the tourists have children with them, they'll grasp their hands tightly as they walk on. I haven't been there for years. None of us put those white daisies in the jar. Or did you? Did you leave those flowers there, and then stand looking down for a long time, thinking thoughts it's too late to uncover now?

I can almost see you. If I turn my head to the black splash of shade under the yew, now, quickly, I'm certain I'll see you. It's noon, the white hour when ghosts walk, leaving no shadow. But I don't turn my head.

There's always a breeze up here. The graveyard is like the deck of a ship, tilted above the land and sailing. If I shut my eyes I can believe I feel the ground shiver. One after another the graves have been stroked down by the wind so that they lean, and then topple, and it's hard to read them. But your stone is new and it'll take time for the wind to bend it. I still can't believe that you are here, near enough to touch if you weren't covered. I can't believe that if I dug down I would find first the quilting of earth, then the box, then you, yourself.

I lie down. I shut my eyes. I am in bed with you, warm with the warmth of night. I feel your long slender legs curled up behind me, your knees digging into my back.

'Go to sleep.'

'I *am* asleep.'

'How can you be asleep when you're talking to me?'

And then silence. We are both asleep, tipping into the valley of the big double bed. My legs are wrapped carefully around with sheets because I can't bear the touch of the mattress's navy-and-white striped ticking, through which poke the sharp ends of feathers. You help me to cover my legs each night.

'Are you sure you can't see any skin?'

'Sure.'

We are both asleep. None of this has happened yet.

I am on your grave, the warm mound of it shaped to me like a body. But though I listen and listen, there's no heartbeat. Your silence begins to soothe me. I could talk to you now, losing my words in the long grass, but it doesn't seem to matter. All the questions I am desperate to ask you float off, as the world floats off just before sleep.

Chapter Two

I should have let the taxi take me all the way up to the house. I've packed more than usual, because I don't know how long I'll be staying, and the weather might change. I've brought some work stuff too – sketch pads, pencils, charcoal, inks. But only one camera. It feels strange to travel without my camera bag, the one I don't dare let out of my sight for a second. In London, at home, I haul it between the sweaty filth of tube trains and the heat of flats, shops and offices. For weeks now it's been the hottest summer I can remember.

I like the early mornings and the smell when the pavement is being hosed down outside cafés. I drink coffee at six and I'm out by seven when the sun's fresh on my arms, water drips from petunias in lamp-post baskets, and vans whizz about full of new bread and newspapers with the print still damp on them. Then I know why I live in London. I'm on my way to meet someone for breakfast and what might just be a new, exciting piece of work. But by eleven the city's used up and sweaty, and the new project's turned out to be photographing someone's summer playscheme for a community newspaper. I'm pushing at invisible barriers all the time, never quite getting the work I really want. What is it my pictures don't do?

No need to think about that now. I shift my bag to the other hand and keep on up the track. It's getting dark and all the white things look whiter still: the tall stiff flowers in the hedge, the moths and my skirt. The air smells unnaturally sweet. There are owls here, but I haven't seen one. Isabel knows about them. *A pair of barn-owls is nesting this year.*

In a way it's lucky I've got so much to carry, or I'd be running and then I'd arrive just the way I don't want to arrive, hot and out of breath and anxious. And then Richard would be angry. *Isabel can't cope with other people's emotions just now,* he said. She's not supposed to know he told me to come. She won't like it; she'll say it's because it's interrupting my life and making me lose commissions when I've worked so hard to build things up. As if I would want to be anywhere else but with her.

I was in the bath when the phone rang. I heard his voice cutting through the answerphone message: 'Nina, if you're there, pick up the phone. It's Richard, it's important.' He knew I often left the answerphone on while I was working. I jumped out of the bath and grabbed the mobile and a towel, and covered myself even though he couldn't see me.

'What's the matter? Is Izzy all right?'

'For God's sake, Nina, calm down.'

'Has she had the baby?'

'Yes, she's had the baby.'

'How is she, what is it, I mean —'

'A boy. It's a boy.'

'A boy.'

I clutched the phone and drips of water ran down it. Isabel has a son. Even as I said the words to myself she grew older, more distant, passing through a door that swung shut in my face.

'Yes. But I'm afraid it didn't go quite as we hoped.' I heard the tension in his voice now, in its curious flatness. I had imagined how I'd get this news so many times. Always it was Isabel phoning me, Isabel with the baby curled in her arm, both of them weary, but triumphant that they'd found one another at last.

I was glad it was a boy, not a girl. I hadn't let myself know before now how much I didn't want Isabel to have a daughter.

'What's happened?'

'I can't go into it all now. I'm at the hospital and they're going to let me see her soon.'

6

'Richard, why's she in hospital? She was going to have it at home.' I heard my own voice, stupidly accusing.

'Well, she didn't. Her uterus ruptured. They just got the baby out in time,' he snapped, as if it was my fault. I was silent, trying to work out what these words mean. *Uterus. Ruptured.*

'You mean she had a Caesarean?'

'I mean she had a hysterectomy.'

'Jesus.'

We were silent. I thought of the wooden hand-made rocking cradle, a stupid extravagance for one child.

'It was all going fine,' he said, 'just as she thought it would. She wasn't even lying down. The midwife was there, having a cup of tea with us while Isabel put some baby clothes to air. She couldn't keep still, she kept moving round.' He paused. 'That track,' he said. 'I'll make Wilkinson surface that effing track if it's the last thing I do.'

Wilkinson is the farmer who owns their house. 'Couldn't the ambulance get down it?' I asked.

'There wasn't time to wait for an ambulance. I drove and the midwife went in the back of the car with her.'

'But she's all right,' I stated. It wasn't bathwater on the phone now, it was sweat from my hands.

'She'll be all right,' said Richard. He threw the monosyllables at me as if they were balls he was bowling too fast. But cricket isn't Richard's game. Richard is three-quarters Irish by blood. Maybe you'd guess it from his eyes, which are bluer than English eyes, and they go with dark hair and skin rather than English fairness. Or you'd guess it from a concentration in his features, which makes them look as if they've been pushed together. He's a big man, over six foot tall and bulky too. He makes me jump when I come on him suddenly in the house.

I didn't know the right questions to ask. I don't know anything about birth, or babies. I listened to the telephone silence and told myself that Isabel was safe in hospital, being looked

7

after. No one dies of having a baby nowadays, even if things go wrong. In a few days she'd be home.

I could smell the hospital, as if I were there too. I saw Isabel flat out on one of those trolleys, her face knocked sideways by pain and her eyes closed. Her stomach was hollow where they'd taken out the baby. Her womb had gone too, that grown-up thing that bled three years before mine did. The wheels squeaked and two men shoved her down the corridor, very fast, towards a lift. In the doorway behind, dwindling, Richard watched too. I knew how he would look angry, and helpless too.

'I'll come down,' I said, 'I can be there in less than three hours.'

'There's no point in you coming now. I'd planned to have this week off anyway. But I'm in Korea next week and she'll need someone then. She'll only just be out of hospital.'

My mouth opened to ask him if he couldn't cancel the trip to Korea, and then shut again. Richard is an economist who specializes in developing computerized models for fast-growth economies. There is not much work for him in Europe. Apparently he is accomplished, single-minded and indispensable in his field. I haven't heard this from Isabel, who never talks about Richard's work, but from an article in the *Financial Times* which said that if Maynard Keynes were reborn now he would be Richard.

'Of course I'll come. I'll come whenever Isabel needs me.'

'Good.'

My hands shook as I jabbed the phone's aerial down into its skull and put it on its rest. I had a pain in my throat, as if talking to Richard had hurt me. I found I was clutching my towel tightly round me. Deliberately, I unclenched my fingers and let it fall. There was my stomach, pale and whole. I thought of Isabel's brown summer belly, her deep navel. I touched my skin and ran my hand across it to feel that it was unscarred. Then I went straight into the kitchen, cut a thick crust of a fresh white loaf, smeared it with butter and then with apricot jam, and ate it fast, cramming it into my mouth. There was sweat on my forehead so I wiped it off and kept on eating. I was not going to let myself think of the things Richard had said, not yet.

It's nearly a mile up the track from the road to Isabel's house. By now I'm walking more slowly, prolonging the moment of not having arrived yet. Usually I do this because I find that holding myself back from something I long for only adds to the pleasure I get in the end. But this time the reason is different. I'm afraid I'll make a mistake. Say the wrong thing, touch her when she doesn't want to be touched, admire the baby when all she cares about is the other babies, the ones she can't have any more. I can be clumsy sometimes. Richard makes me feel that I am clumsy most of the time. There is too much of me for him.

And then I see it. An owl, its wings spread, going down the lane in front of me. So light, it reminds me

'The way some birds fly, you'd think they were fucking the air.'

Who said that? I can't remember. Someone I didn't expect to have thoughts like that, because I was surprised.

The owl will get there first. I shift my case to the other hand yet again, and plod on.

Chapter Three

But when I get there, Isabel's asleep. Richard is outside on the broad stone step, sitting on a kitchen chair, a glass of beer in his hand. I see him first not even as a person but as a bulk in the summer gloom, barring the entrance to the house. I get closer and the shadows resolve into Richard, like a puzzle picture. There's his paper collapsed into a tent beside the chair.

'She's asleep,' he says as soon as he sees me. 'Better wait till morning now. I didn't think you were coming so late.'

'I had to see someone. It went on longer than I expected.' As usual I'm aware of how feeble my world seems when Richard's cuts across it. He believes that any meeting which lasts longer than an hour is a waste of time.

'I saw that picture of yours,' he says abruptly. 'In the *Telegraph*, wasn't it?'

'The magazine,' I say, too quickly.

'Interesting subject.'

It was a travellers' wedding over in Ireland, and I'd been there with someone who knew the bridegroom. I'd felt out of place at first, with the drinking and dancing. I don't drink when I'm working, and I don't dance either, or not often, not easily. I knew no one there, not even the man who'd brought me, really, but I got talking to some children, a crowd of them sitting on the steps of a trailer. They wanted to look at the camera, the way kids always do. I had a Polaroid with me too, and that made things easy. Even these days, people often don't want their photos taken, or else they want something back for it, money or other things. I liked that wedding and it showed in the pictures. I liked the way they'd spent money they hadn't got, and the children were wise to what was going on, the drinking and the fights breaking out, but loving it too, innocently, in the way children can do two things at once. There was a little girl who held out her hand to me for money and one of the other girls slapped her hand down because I'd given each of them their photograph to keep already. She didn't slap her hard, just a little slap to show she knew what manners were. I took out a ten-pound note and folded it small and wrapped her hand round it and the big girl said she'd make sure her Mammy kept it for her.

'It was good,' says Richard. 'Good composition.'

I smile in the dark. Normally I don't like it when people who don't know the subject use its terminology, but tonight I'm touched that he bothered to notice the picture and tell me that it was good. It seems a good omen.

Behind us the house is silent. 'Where's the baby?'

'He's with Susan. Oh, I forgot, you probably don't know about Susan. Susan Wilkinson. She's just finished an NNEB and she can help Isabel out for a couple of months. She's sleeping here the first couple of weeks, but once Isabel's better she'll come every day and sleep at home. Just as well. She's getting on my nerves already.'

'Is she good with the baby?'

'She's very good.'

We say 'the baby' as we did before he was born. He has a name, but to me it doesn't sound like a baby's name. He is called Antony. Much later, when it can't possibly sound like a criticism, I'll ask Isabel how they came to choose it.

'I'll go in,' I say. He looks up but only moves aside half a foot or so, and I have to step round him, into the kitchen which smells old and cool and slightly fusty, as if it's a long time since anyone's cooked here. I pull the string and the light comes on. It's a big room, floored in stone with a few dirty rag rugs which were here before Isabel came. Then there's an electric cooker which looks too small for the room, and cupboards, lots of cupboards in which there are sometimes mouse droppings.

There is a square table marked by knives, on which there's a heap of gooseberries in a wooden colander. A range which is never used crouches against one wall. The Wilkinsons lived here in the farmhouse once, before they made enough money selling a hundred acres when land prices were high to build themselves the house of their dreams, two fields away. Once I thought I'd like to make a collage from images of these two houses, like two hands of cards dealt together, but then I knew it would be too easy, and too obvious. Mrs Wilkinson has a fitted kitchen in pale buffed oak. She has good taste.

I love this room. To me it seems entirely beautiful, in the same way as my sister seem entirely beautiful, and yet it makes me angry. I almost don't want to see it. If this is beautiful, if it calls out in me that small almost sexual shiver I can't fake, then what does that say about my white-walled attic flat with its windows set in at odd angles, showing other people's chimney-pots and tiles? I could no more make a kitchen like Isabel's than I could fly through the air.

Isabel doesn't own the house. She has it on a lease from the Wilkinsons, who sometimes speak of how they'll do it up for their sons when they marry. I've seen Margery Wilkinson drink her cup of tea in here and look round appraisingly at a window to be double-glazed, or a row of shelves to be torn out. But Isabel lives here as if she'll live here for ever. That was why she wanted to have the baby in this house, upstairs, in her own bed, so that he'd first open his eyes here. I suppose Richard might want to buy a house, but Isabel won't leave here until she's forced out. He must have known that when he married her.

Richard comes in, yawning. He throws the paper on the table and takes a bottle of whisky out of a cupboard, and two small glasses. I shake my head. It's one of the few drinks I don't like.

'You might as well,' he says. 'There's not much chance of a decent night's sleep otherwise.'

'Does he cry a lot?'

'I don't know what they're supposed to do, but he seems to cry most of the night, yes. And then there's Susan pattering about in her pyjamas, so it's hardly restful. She sees no reason why I should sleep while she and Isabel are awake.'

I take the offered glass. He pours whisky in, not too much, and again I'm pleased. The whisky tastes disgusting, as usual. He pours himself another immediately.

'That bloody girl's got religion as well,' he says.

'What, Susan?'

'Mm. She went off to some Jesus camp in the summer and she's never stopped talking about it since. God help the children she gets her hands on. She's going to be a nanny, you know.'

'Well, you don't need to worry about the baby yet.'

'No, I suppose not. But it's a bore for Isabel . . .' He frowns. 'On top of the baby and everything else.'

I look at him. At that moment I realize that I've been wrong all the time, ever since Isabel first told me she was pregnant. It was an accident, she said, her lids half-closed, smiling slightly. She sounded unworried, but cool, and of course I believed her. I'm in the habit of believing Isabel's version. It was as deliberate a composition as a photograph of a begging child, alone on a barren street, carefully angled to exclude the mother three yards away. It wasn't Richard who had wanted the baby, it was Isabel. What Richard wanted was their life together as it had been before, with no extra presences forced on them. First Susan Wilkinson, and now me. And the baby. He'd do his best for the baby because that was the kind of man he was, but he would have preferred to be alone with Isabel. He didn't mind that there would be no more children.

I know how he feels, because it is how I feel myself.

I hold out my glass, and he pours in more whisky. The whisky burns a hole in my stomach, as a magnifying glass burns into grass on a hot day. I lean back against the wall and the alcohol skids into my veins.

'You'll see her in the morning,' Richard goes on, unfolding the paper, refolding it with the pages in the right order. 'I'll be off at six, so I shan't see you.'

'Oh.'

'Tell Susan I'm back on Friday. I've cut the trip short. She might have forgotten, she's a bit dozy. I've given her a list of phone numbers to pass on to you. Any problem, ring me.'

'Of course I will,' I say too quickly, too airily, for he slaps me down. 'I mean it. If she's not well again, don't start thinking you can cope. Get on to me right away.'

He is massive, more adult and more experienced than I can ever be. But he sways slightly, his head down, like an animal being baited by something just out of sight. On the other side of this cold wall there's a corridor, and then a staircase, and at the top there are seven doors. Behind one of them there's Isabel, sleeping now. Their bedroom with its smell of marriage which vanishes as soon as Richard goes, and becomes the smell of Isabel again. Her skin, her hair, her oatmeal soap in her bedroom wash-basin, and the clothes she's taken off hanging on the back of the door. She wears one scent all the time, and although I like it myself I would never buy it. I've sprayed it on myself in department stores sometimes, and for a few seconds I've become someone else. Not quite Isabel. I'm bad at scents and make-up, bad at clothes. It took me years to realize that it might be easier to do things like shave my legs or make an appointment at a good hairdresser's than not to do them. It's always seemed so complicated to me, being a woman. I hear other women talking about 'my size' and 'what suits me', swopping tales of smears and tests and samples. I'd like to be that confident. I'd like to believe those things were part of me, and I was part of them. Maybe that's why it suits me to take pictures. No one looks at the person behind the camera.

But I did a series of self-portraits once. It was hard to begin with, but it got easier. In one I was naked. Not naked the way I'd want anyone else to see me, not posing naked or sex naked. Just naked. It was a strange thing to do and at the time I had no idea why I was doing it. But it worked. All the things that make me uneasy broke down into grains of black and white. What I needed to think about were the technicalities. In the end I quite liked looking at those shapes, those angles, and what the light had done. I did justice to my own flesh and blood.

I wonder if Isabel's really asleep.

Chapter Four

I'm awake at five. I want to pee but I hear Richard moving about, water rushing, doors opening and closing, and then a thin, startled sound which I don't identify straight away. Of course, the baby. It cries hectically, then suddenly stops. The light is soft and grey. I've left my curtains open. This side of the house doesn't look out over Isabel's garden, but over the pond and the barns. A family of ducks sails out, the ducklings bobbing with minute confidence in their mother's wake. There's grey dew on the grass where the ducks have walked and left their footprints.

A door slams downstairs. Richard, going. I hear his footsteps crunch round to the patch of gravel where they keep their car. I lean out, feeling the cool on my arms, still wanting to pee. The car door clunks, the engine turns, the tyres spit gravel and he's gone. I listen for a long time to the whine of the engine going down the track slowly, in second gear.

I step out into the corridor. There's no sign of Susan and no sound of the baby now. Isabel's door is closed. I go into the bathroom where a huge mahogany-seated lavatory squats by the bath. I pee quietly, and pull the long chain. Water roars over the crazed porcelain, sluicing the name *Victrix*. Water seethes in the cistern, and then silence replaces noise again. They must all be asleep. I look at my watch. Five past six.

I wash my face and hands in cold chalky water, and then creep back to the bedroom, pull on my jeans and the red tank top I've washed out and dried overnight. It's damp, but that feels nice. It's going to be hot again. There is heat everywhere this summer, rolled up overnight like a blanket. I could go out. To the garden, perhaps, to see how it's changed since I was here last time. Or through the farmyard on to the thread of a path that leads up to the Downs. But I'm here to look after Isabel, who may be sleeping or may be lying down flat on her back, staring out of the window, a single vertical line cut into her forehead. That line comes when she has pain. I step back into the corridor, tasting its cool smooth boards with my bare feet.

'Nina? Nina, is that you?'

Our mother wouldn't let us shout from room to room. 'If you want to say something to Isabel, go and find her first.' I remember staring in wonder at a schoolfriend who bawled 'Mu – um! I'm home!' as she opened the front door. If we wanted to speak to our mother, we could go in and speak to her. We rarely did. The door of her studio was shut, and behind it she was working. If we went in she would glance up, her slippery hands controlling the live clay by touch, and most of the things we were going to say would seem not worth saying.

'Nina?'

I open the door. There she is, sitting up in bed. 'Isabel!'

'Come on in, darling. Shut the door or I'll have Susan back again.'

She smiles, putting the paper she's writing on to one side, but keeping the pen in her hand. She's got her reading glasses on, the wire-rimmed ones she got in a second-hand shop. She can see through them perfectly, she says. I go up to the bed, feel myself smiling down at her, a big, speechless smile that stretches wider and wider until I don't know what to do with it. Isabel holds out one hand and lifts her face to be kissed, shutting her eyes.

I kiss her gingerly, on the cheek. She's smooth and warm as always, but I'm afraid to jolt her and start up the pain which I know is hidden somewhere under the bedclothes. She opens her eyes and screws up her nose.

'That wasn't much of a kiss. Lovely top, Nina. You ought to wear colours like that more, instead of all that black.'

I glance down at what she's writing. Three or four sheets of it, closely covered. She sees me looking and says, 'I was writing to Edward. He's coming to stay the day after tomorrow. He and Alex have had another bust-up.'

I stare at Isabel. 'Hasn't he got more sense than to come here now, when you're still ill? Who does he think's going to look after him?'

She smiles and shrugs. 'You know Edward. He doesn't take much looking after. He just wants to get away for a while and try to work out what to do. I had a long letter from him yesterday.'

'Does Richard know?'

'Of course.'

When I first came in I thought she looked well, but now I can see how pallid she is under her usual summer tan. Isabel doesn't easily show tiredness, or illness. She shifts her legs under the cotton cover.

'I'm supposed to keep doing these exercises,' she explains, 'to stop getting blood clots. It's lucky no one tells you about all this beforehand. I shouldn't tell *you*.' There's this fiction between us, that I might start wanting children some day.

'Is it all healing up OK?' I ask cautiously. Isabel laughs.

'Don't worry, Neen, I'm not going to show you. It's not as bad as you'd think. The midwife says I'm a good healer.'

When she was pregnant Isabel talked about the midwife a lot. *Midwife* sounded like one of those words which ought to be archaic, but isn't. I imagined her earthy, full of wisdom, her eyes kind, her hands cool, her hair streaked with grey: the way Isabel wanted her to be, perhaps. But I met her once and she was a wispy fair girl driving a Ford Fiesta. Isabel and I were in the habit of exaggerating our own lives, and each other's. I was London, a series of small flats with someone living below who played 'Do You Really Love Me?' with the speakers hanging out of the windows, and my phone ringing at midnight. I was work and safe sex but lots of it and cruising the streets for a late-night chemist, and crises and spending too much money, and being dissatisfied. What Isabel was took longer to explain. All this began as a game we played, the kind of game sisters play when they need to find out how different they are. But it turned into a game that played us.

'I don't mind if you show me,' I say.

Isabel raises her eyebrows. She pushes down the cover, and pulls up her nightdress. 'They've just taken off the dressing and the clips,' she says. She's right, it's not as bad as I'd imagined. The scar is a reddish-purple line, with what look like rows of teethmarks above and below it. 'That's where the clips were,' says Isabel, 'and that's where they put in the drain.' She looks down at her scar, absorbed. 'They keep going on about how I'll still be able to wear a bikini.'

Her pubic hair has been shaved off and there are deep bruises on her stomach. 'The things they think of,' she says.

'What's he like?'

A secretive expression crosses Isabel's face. I know it well. She always looked like this when she first made a new friend whom she didn't want me to meet. 'Not at all like I expected,' she says. 'You'll see.'

'I can't wait to see him.'

'It's wonderful when he's asleep. Susan's taken him because it's too light in here. He thinks it's morning. But I'll have to feed him again at seven.' She frowns and pushes her glasses back up her nose.

'Just tell me what you want doing. I've come to help.'

Isabel's face lightens. 'Oh Neen, I've been thinking about it half the night. You know I'd put in three new apple trees in that bed at the bottom of the south wall? Richard won't have watered them, and they need gallons in this weather. Could you run the hose down there and let them soak?'

'Of course,' I say. And then, 'It's a pity Richard took the car. I could easily have driven him to the airport and then we'd have had it while he was away.'

'I didn't even think of it,' says Isabel, 'I keep forgetting you can drive.' I can drive, Isabel can't. I learned five years ago when I started getting commissions which meant travel.

'It's only a mile and a bit into the village as the bee flies,' says Isabel.

'Not as the pram pushes,' I point out.

'He won't be in a pram. I've got a sling.'

'But you've *got* a pram, haven't you?' That was one of my plans, that I'd take the baby for long walks in his pram while Isabel slept. I've never pushed a pram, and I quite liked the idea of it.

'I haven't bothered. Where would Susan push it, down the track and back again? We'll sort out something once Richard gets back.'

But she has piles of clothes, collected here and there, plain white nightgowns and hand-knitted cardigans. She has even embroidered tiny ducks and apples on them herself. When I was here last I watched her embroidering, a new skill for her long quick fingers.

Isabel leans back suddenly. 'I'm so tired,' she says suddenly, in a voice wrenched from some place she refuses to show me.

'I'll go. I'll let you sleep.'

'Don't go yet.' She shuts her eyes. They shut tight, the lids sealed over the globes of her eyes. Her face is thinner, but her breasts are round and hard as stones under the thin lawn of her nightdress. The pen she's dropped is staining the bed cover. Without saying anything I pick it up, and the sheets of paper. *Richard feels* . . . I read. I put the papers on her bedside table.

'Can I get you anything?'

Her head moves on the pillow, side to side, slowly. No. One of her hands creeps towards me, an inch or two, palm upturned. I take it and fold it in mine.

'I'll just sit here, then,' I say quietly, and I think she smiles. I sit still, holding Isabel's hand. Her bed is placed so that someone sitting up in bed looks straight out over the garden, and then beyond the garden wall to the meadows and the line of the Downs. I can see a tree with red fruit on it that seems to drip down the stone of the wall. There are cattle moving into one of the meadows, a long line of them, seeming to go by themselves at this distance. But then I hear a faint cry through the window, a man's voice, driving the cattle. And another cry, not faint at all, answering it from inside the house. The baby. Even on me it acts like sandpaper jagging over my skin. I feel Isabel tense. I look down and see two rings rise like jumping fish, one over each nipple. Her milk. She turns and opens her eyes, begins to raise herself awkwardly on one elbow.

'Tell Susan to bring him in. I don't want him to cry.'

Next to Isabel Susan looks indecently healthy. Her short fair curls brush Isabel's cheek as she leans down with the baby, putting him with what looks like exaggerated care into Isabel's arms. He is purple all over, arms and legs wagging feebly as he feels himself let down through the air. He butts into Isabel and screams.

'He can smell the milk,' says Susan in a loud voice. A fight breaks out between Isabel's breast and the baby, who doesn't seem to know what to do with it. 'He's not latched on! He's not latched on!' shouts Susan.

'All *right*,' says Isabel in a low, furious voice. The baby dives towards her navel, his head wobbling. The struggle begins again, the baby screaming louder than ever, Susan forcing his head up, a film of sweat appearing on Isabel's forehead. Suddenly there is silence.

'Jesus Christ,' says Isabel. The baby sucks noisily, his purple colour draining to pink. Susan stands back, and slowly Isabel's free hand comes around the baby, and her two middle fingers begin to tap his back.

'Ooh, we've started him off on the wrong side, I never realized,' says Susan.

'Well he's not bloody coming off now,' says Isabel, with her eyes shut.

'Shall I make you a cup of tea?' I suggest. I catch a glint of a glance from Isabel. 'Susan'll make it. She knows where everything is,' she says firmly, and Susan goes off with a crisp, bright tread which somehow manages to be reproachful, too.

'It's not like that when she's not here,' says Isabel.

'It looked . . .' I fumble for the right words, 'extraordinary.'

Isabel laughs. 'Have a proper look at him now she's gone. Do you like him?'

I look at him. Now he is calm I can see he's fair. He even has a light lick of hair. His eyes are screwed shut.

'He's such a big baby. I thought he'd be tiny and dark,' says Isabel.

Tiny and dark, like I was. Isabel can remember that.

'He doesn't look much like Richard,' I say.

'No,' says Isabel, but she's only half listening now. One finger touches the sole of a dangling purple foot, which kicks convulsively. She looks inward, and remote. I remember suddenly how she would turf my baby out of the doll's pram we shared, in order to lay hers there.

'I want you to take pictures of him,' she says.

Chapter Five

I'm under the fig tree, with its big leaves all round me like hands to keep off the sun. There are plenty of figs this year, and for once they're going to ripen. Their warm, spicy smell fills the shade where I sit. It's half-past two, and the sky's white with heat. In this weather you sit out the glare, waiting for the long light of evening. But I don't mind, not here, not miles from London where the only sound of traffic is the distant hoot of a train as it gets to the level crossing, and there's no one crowding into my shade. The shadow of the fig leaves is extraordinarily sharp, almost more distinct than the thing itself. I put out my foot, let the edge of shadow cut it, draw it back again.

From here you can't see the house, and the house can't see you. Or rather, no one in the house can see me now. I count them up. Susan, in her glory this afternoon because the health visitor's coming at three. Isabel, who must be there too. Edward, who lay in bed most of the morning, recovering, and has probably gone back there again after eating a good lunch. Recovering from what? Too much sex between the wrong people, that's all it comes down to, though he and Isabel have turned it into something else which puts out its feelers all over the house. Every time I come into a room there he is, Edward, moody on a footstool, his chin on his hands, explaining to Isabel the enigma which is himself. He stops when he sees me. Edward has an actor's instinct for a good audience.

Susan's scented danger. Edward is a serious distraction from the business of baby. She tried sending him off on a mission to get a particular type of nappy-rash cream yesterday, and even had a small list made out for him of things he might as well get while he was there. Edward doesn't drive, either, so this involved two changes of bus. It would have kept him out of the house for several hours. Edward didn't say no. He never says no. He smiled at Susan, and waited until she went away again.

The baby sleeps. That baby sleeps with his whole heart. I'm getting to like watching him, the patterns he makes across his white flannelette sheets, the way he flings himself down the current of sleep, his lips pursed, his face so smooth there seem to be no features in it at all. Or perhaps just the perfect dab of his nose, at some angles. I look at him for a long time, but I haven't taken any pictures yet, or tried to draw him. It's hard to get in to see him alone. He is Isabel's. I don't want to draw the curve of her arm around him, or the way her neck bends, or his legs curling to her breast. He's often naked while she feeds him, because it's so hot. Isabel's offering me these things all the time, but I don't want them. I know them already.

And of course there's more to it than that. Of course I'm jealous. But of whom?

I've brought out a sketchbook. Just a little one, the paper the size of a postcard. That's the kind of drawing I want to do, drawings done as if through a keyhole, so that the way the image is framed becomes as important as the image itself. But my eye's out. I don't draw enough. You have to draw every day, every single day, if you want to keep your eye in. And your hand, and all the other things. My mother was the first person who taught me to draw. When I got angry with myself and crumpled things up she'd say, 'It doesn't matter. Better to do a drawing than not do one, even if it's no good. Because of that bad drawing you'll be able to do a better one tomorrow.' She had no time for people who wanted everything they did to be perfect. I can remember it now, sitting in her studio facing the tumble of roofs above the beach. Only it wasn't a tumble once you looked at it. Every roof related precisely to space and the tilt of the land. I can hear her say, 'You have to *look* at it, Nina.' And then her hand came over my shoulder, took a piece of paper, drew quickly.

'That's only the way I see it,' she said. Her hands were long like Isabel's, but much rougher. You could see she worked with her hands. 'In fact I think you'll draw better than I do, in the end, if you keep at it.'

I'm going to draw that cabbage, there, that fat, loose one squatting in a bed of big poppies. I'm going to do it quickly, without thinking about it too much. I flip to a new page, hold my pencil like a cutting tool, and begin.

He doesn't surprise me. When you're looking so hard, you notice every change of light, and his shadow is big, like him. He's still in a suit.

'I thought I'd find some shade here,' he says. 'You don't mind if I join you?'

I move along the wooden bench, closing the sketchbook. 'No, of course not.'

'I've stopped you working,' he says. 'I didn't want to do that.'

I glance up, pleased and surprised. 'I'll go back to it,' I say. 'Is the health visitor still there?'

'I haven't been in yet,' says Richard.

He looks tired, his dark skin sallow. 'There was a crowd of them in the bedroom,' he says. 'I'll go into Isabel once she's alone. I rang from the airport.'

'Edward's here.'

'Yes, I thought he very probably would be.'

'Alex might be coming down at the weekend, too.'

Richard doesn't answer. He stares out over the garden, his eyes narrowed against the glare.

'And here you are drawing a cabbage,' he says.

'I'm perfectly happy,' I say, and it's true. He turns and looks at me, then says, 'I've never seen it before, but you do look like your mother, don't you? There's a photo of her working which looks just like you did just then.'

'You never saw my father, either.'

'No. I'd like to have met him. Isabel was very fond of him.'

'He was very selfish,' I say suddenly, without meaning to. 'I didn't realize it until he was dead. It was impossible to think that while you were with him.'

'Isabel says your mother was selfish. Before she had the baby she said all she'd have to do was think of what your mother did with you two, and then do the opposite.'

He looks at me closely. I wonder if we are talking about my parents still, or about me and Isabel. 'I know she thinks that,' I say, 'but it would have been different if she'd been interested in what my mother did.'

'You say "my mother", so does Isabel. Not "our mother".'

'We see her differently.'

Part of me itches for him to go, so that I can pick up the pencil again. I can see another, better way of drawing the cabbage now. But on the other hand, this is the least awkward conversation I've ever had with Richard.

'The baby looks a bit like him,' I say abruptly.

'Who?'

'My father. Our father. His grandfather,' I say, discovering this fact suddenly. The baby is not just Isabel's. It is knitted into a chain of resemblances.

'It amazes me how people find resemblances in babies,' says Richard.

'I suppose it's what you look for.'

He frowns, as if impatient. He wants to be with Isabel, not here. He's counting the moments until he hears the health visitor's car go down the track, until he can see Isabel on his own.

'I'm starving,' he says. 'The food on the plane was inedible.'

'There's some gooseberry pie in the fridge.'

'You couldn't get me some, could you, Nina? I don't want to bump into that woman.'

'Well . . .' I say, my hand reaching for the sketchbook which I am not going to leave with him, 'all right.'

He smiles, his eyes going into their creases. Richard is forty-six, older, heavier, weightier than us. 'Good,' he says. I stand up and walk out of the shade into the glare of the sun, up one of Isabel's little paths. She has planted low box hedges to contain the profusion that loops through trees, over trellises, up walls and around doorways. I like that dark, firm green. I like the way these hedges pinch the sense that there is too much of everything here. It's very like Isabel, who is beautiful enough to wear reading glasses which most women would throw away.

I find the pie under a plate. Edward has been at it since lunch, digging out the fruit, which he prefers to the crust. I cut a straight line across the spoiled part, and then a thick wedge, the right size for Richard. There's some cream in a jug, thick and yellow. Susan's mother sent the pie over, and it has a spray of elderflower in it to bring out the taste of the gooseberries. She has patterned the crust with pastry leaves. The inside of the crust is white and glutinous now the pastry has cooled, and cooking has thinned the skin of the berries so the seeds show through it. I pick one out, fragile but still whole, and eat it. I am hungry too. I cut another piece of the pie, for myself, and pour cream over them both, take two spoons and shake some sugar from a caster over the cream. I can hear voices, but the baby has stopped crying. A door opens and the voices grow louder. They must be coming out. I pick up the plates and hurry out into the light, round the corner by the pond and into the garden.

Richard hasn't moved, except to take off his shoes and socks. He lies back with his feet in the sun, eyes shut. His feet are pale, naked-looking, city feet.

'Here you are.'

We dig into the crust, the cream, the fruit. The edges of the cream are just beginning to swim in the heat already. I've always liked eating with Richard, because he is greedy, as I am. You can always tell. He leaves the plumpest gooseberry until last, to duck

27

it in its own pond of cream. The sugar grits pleasantly on my teeth.

'I should have brought the rest of it,' I say. 'Edward'll only eat it otherwise.'

Wasps are on the empty plates already. 'Better go in,' says Richard, weighing, picking up his shoes.

'I didn't hear the car.'

'Didn't you? I did. You were lost in that pie.'

'I'll come later,' I say. The cabbage has changed slightly, wilted a little in the afternoon heat.

'If she stood at the window, and I stood on the path, just by those sweet williams, I could see her,' says Richard. 'She often looks at the garden from there.'

'She hasn't been out. It's too hot for the baby.'

'He'll have to get used to it,' says Richard, 'Isabel lives in this garden.'

But she hasn't been in it since I got here. Edward doesn't like the sun, either, and their long talks go on indoors, in Isabel's room, or in the shaded, stuffy, downstairs sitting-room. I couldn't have imagined the garden without Isabel before this summer. She knew it, she planted it, she was always moving in it somewhere, or else she'd have left a trowel, a tray of cuttings, a ball of string to show that she'd be back soon. But the garden goes on without her, though I know it's an illusion. It'll rot from the inside, like pears left too long in a bowl.

But it's perfect now, and this afternoon it feels as much mine as anyone's. I move back deeper into the shade of the fig tree. I think that I'll draw a fig next, the bare knob of it stuck to its silvery branch. Everything around me seems to have grown on its own, flaring into colour or fading like those delphiniums which are bleached ghosts of themselves now. Drawing is easier when I can't see Isabel's long hands everywhere, in the soil, among the leaves, parting clumps of flowers, cutting, nicking, grafting, taking away.

Chapter Six

'You don't look very alike,' Susan said yesterday. 'I wouldn't have guessed you were sisters.'

She had the baby in her arms. He'd been miserable all day after crying half the night, and Isabel was exhausted. The wound wasn't healing where the drain had been, Susan said. She was going to phone the doctor later. Isabel was resting while Richard sat with her in the big armchair, going through papers. I had cooked a chicken to eat cold for supper, and dug up new potatoes. They'd been white as eggs when they came out of the earth but they were skinning over now, already brown. Later, just before we ate, I'd pull some lettuce.

'I like those shorts,' said Susan. 'I think it's nice, the way everyone wears shorts now.'

I looked down at my legs, and laughed. They were far from perfect but I liked them.

'She's beautiful, isn't she?' said Susan, staring at me intently as if she really didn't know the answer.

'Yes, she is,' I answered, and Susan sighed.

'Never mind,' I said, 'we don't all have to look like that.'

She grinned back. For the first time we were nearly liking one another. 'I haven't got a sister,' she said, 'just brothers. Great lumps playing at cricket the whole time. Everyone's mad about cricket round here.'

'There were just the two of us,' I said.

'Yes, but you were the artistic one, weren't you?' she went on, following a train of thought that led from Isabel's beauty.

'I take photographs, and I draw. I don't call myself an artist.'

'You do lovely drawings. I've always wanted to be able to draw.' As she said it I saw her as a little girl, leaning breathily over the shoulder of a school friend. 'Ooh, yours is brilliant! Mine's rubbish.' But I couldn't be bothered to give Susan the contradictions she wanted. I smiled vaguely and wiped my earthy hands on my shorts.

I keep thinking about Isabel. Being in the same house for so long is working strangely, making me think of her more rather than less. I think of us being sisters. She's like me, more like me than Susan sees, and yet not like. All those genes thrown up into the air as casually as dice have come down quite differently each time. Once I used to think Isabel had had all the sixes, but now I'm not so sure. She's three years older than me, so the family she grew up in was never quite the same as the one I knew. She remembers – or says she remembers – the time before I was born, when she walked between our parents holding a hand of each, linking them. When she talked to our parents about that time in front of me, I seemed to vanish. My not existing was as real to them as my existing. Isabel remembers our mother being pregnant. She was the big one, the sensible one, and I was the toddler who could scream and bite. For years I accepted Isabel's lists of the things I had done to her, not even beginning to think that there might be other lists, other things, done to me. She told her stories with an air of adult patience, for adult ears.

'Nina cut the eyelashes off Rosina. She thought they'd grow again. She doesn't realize Rosina's only a doll.'

But she doesn't tell how every time it was my turn for the doll's pram she would calmly, firmly take out my doll and put in her own.

'You see, Nina, Mandy doesn't fit in the pram properly. Look at her legs sticking out. Rosina came with the pram, so it's hers really. But I'll let you have a turn pushing her.'

And off we went to push our doll's pram round Barnoon Cemetery, up and down the little paths, visiting our favourite graves. Below us the sea glittered and the holiday people threw themselves in and out of the waves, but we took no notice of them. Our parents let us go where we liked. We'd walk as far as Wicca Pool sometimes, and swim with the seals. Once we saw a honeymoon couple bathing there naked, their fronds of pubic hairs touching.

'They'll lie down on the rocks and cuddle each other next,' said Isabel authoritatively, and they did. Isabel was so sure of things that sometimes I thought it was her certainty that made them happen. Without Isabel's predictions I'd have been lost in a world where anything might come next. She even knew when I was going to cry.

Once I slipped when we were running back along the cliff path. We'd been picking blackberries and I was watching the berries bounce in the bucket clasped in front of me, not the path. My foot caught on a stone, and I fell sideways, not safely on to the path, but sliding with horrible smoothness and speed to the lip of the cliff. I saw myself going and heard Isabel scream, and then I went over. But it was a rough slope, not the edge of the cliff itself, which was still fifteen feet away. I slid ten of them, bumping and banging, and then stopped. I began to scream, lying on my back, looking straight up at the sky. A second later a half-circle of terror broke the sky, upside down. It took me a moment to realize that this was Isabel's face. The next minute she was with me, dragging me back with both hands over the scattered blackberries. I got back to the path and sat down on it, shivering. My legs were smeared with blood and blackberry juice. There was a long burning graze up the inside of my arms.

'My bucket's gone,' I said.

'I'll have a look.' Isabel stood up and peered down. 'I can't see it. It must have gone over.'

I thought of my new bucket, silvery inside, bouncing and clanging down to the rocks, and I began to cry. Then Isabel was crying too, worse than me, shaking and hiding her face with her hands. She hardly ever cried, and this was worse than losing the bucket. I patted her shoulders but she didn't seem to feel it. 'It's all right, Isabel. I didn't fall. I'm all right.' But she cried harder and I gave up and began to pick up the fallen blackberries and eat them. I wiped off the dust carefully and popped them into my mouth, one by one. They were delicious. And then there was Isabel, facing me on hands and knees, her face fierce. She was all smeary with crying, but back to herself again.

'And don't you dare tell them, Nina. Or I'll say I told you to stop and you ran on.'

I wonder what Isabel sees when she looks back at the past. We aren't the kind of sisters who talk about their childhood together. If we did we might find we hadn't got many shared memories. And here's Antony, who won't have a brother or a sister at all. No one to cover up for, and no one to betray. Isabel hasn't talked about that. She showed me the scar but she hasn't talked about what the hysterectomy means to her. Now that there are no more baby clothes to embroider she spends hours doing a cross-stitch landscape, while Edward talks to her. I can see Edward loving it: the dip of Isabel's head, the maternity he can enjoy when the baby's not there, the needle flashing in and out. Isabel works quickly, and she listens carefully, looking up at him from time to time, letting him talk himself out. Or they are silent together. I don't like it when I come into her room in the middle of one of their silences.

Richard comes into the kitchen while I'm jointing the chicken.

'How's Isabel?'

'She's trying to sleep. She says she can't settle down while I'm there.'

He pours water into the kettle and plugs it in. 'I'm getting that doctor over. She ought to be feeling better than this by now.'

32

I expect him to go straight out with his coffee, but he sits down in one of the high-backed kitchen chairs.

'Can I give you a hand?'

'You could chop these onions and put them in the salad.'

'What's that you're making?'

'I'm going to do a chicken risotto for Isabel. She might like something hot, we've had a lot of salad.'

'You're a good cook, aren't you?'

'I should be.'

'Why?'

'People who like eating make the best cooks.'

He smiles. 'Have you been drawing again today?'

'Yes, I was out this morning.' I say it quickly, like someone hiding a secret greed. 'I took some pictures too, over at the Wilkinsons'. But it's not my subject. I don't know enough about farming. They're just snaps. Susan's interesting, though. I'd like to do some pictures of Susan when she's working with the baby.'

'I haven't really looked at her,' says Richard. I smile, and cube breast of chicken with one of Isabel's sharp knives.

'Susan's going to be quite something when she gets going,' I say.

'Can't you take some pictures of Isabel? I know she wants you to.'

'Oh, I expect I will. There's plenty of time.'

'It seems a bit of a waste of time photographing Susan. It's not as if she's going to carry on working here. The baby'll never see her again once she goes off to be a nanny.'

'It's what's happening now that interests me,' I say. 'That's what I draw. That's what I photograph. I don't look at a cabbage and say it's not worth drawing because we're going to eat it tomorrow.'

Richard is silent. Then, 'I don't care what you do,' he says rather irritably. 'I was only thinking of Isabel.'

'I know you were.'

I look up from the bowl of fine, moist chicken, and hold his eyes.

'I'm here because you asked me to come,' I say, 'but I'm not just something of Isabel's.'

'I didn't think you were,' he says, looking straight back at me.

I stand up and go to one of the cupboards behind me. I take out green olive oil, arborio rice, a tiny packet of saffron, pine-nuts.

'You've been shopping.'

'Yes, I took your car into Lewes this morning. You remember I asked you if I could use it.'

'Of course you can use it. It's ridiculous the way no one drives it but me. But you've got lots of stuff there – how much do I owe you?'

'I'm staying in your house, eating your food all the time. Anyway, I've got plenty of money at the moment.'

'Have you? Are things going well?'

'I'm charging more than I was. It's going fine.'

It's true. The kind of work I don't really want flows in. Documentary, and a bit banal. One day I got out of the taxi and saw my camera bag still on the floor. I could never afford to replace the stuff. And yet I had to stop myself from paying the fare, turning away, disappearing into the anonymous crowd.

'It's going fine,' I repeat. I'm standing as I say this, pouring a thin stream of oil into Isabel's heaviest pan, looking down on him.

'It's important to make sure you charge enough. Other people judge you by that,' he says.

'Don't worry,' I say. 'Money's important to me.'

'And to me. But then I'm not an artist.'

'Artists don't have to be stupid. My mother wasn't. She was very good with money.'

'I want Isabel to approach Wilkinson again, about buying this

34

house. I could make him the kind of offer he'd think twice about. But she's against it.'

'It would be your house then,' I point out.

'It would be in our joint names.'

'Yes. But the lease is in Isabel's name now.'

'She doesn't like talking about it. She says I knew the situation when we married, which I did. But situations are fluid, they can change.'

This is the first time I've heard Richard say anything remotely critical of Isabel. He's noticed something I thought only I had noticed, that Isabel doesn't like change. She's afraid of it. It's true that she's followed her own path, but having done so she rarely steps off it. And suddenly I feel a wash of tenderness for her, without knowing where this comes from.

Chapter Seven

Beyond Isabel's garden, before the Downs, there are the water-meadows. The river runs through them. All day it's been wrapped in the heat haze that hides the Downs. It's been hot enough for mirages, for rivers walking upside down on air. Isabel says the river is the reason she came here. She was walking along the river, and she saw the house staring at her from its empty windows. She climbed the wall and dropped down into the garden from the branches of a plum tree. Just Isabel, alone in a hot quiet garden which had been empty so long even the birds weren't afraid of her. Everything was matted with bindweed and brambles which would take her two years to clear before she began to plant.

Some winters the river floods the meadows, but now it runs smoothly between its banks, which are raised above the land on either side. There is so much chalk in the water that it turns a pale, opaque green in the sun. Isabel says it's full of chemicals washed off the soil, and though children used to swim in it, they can't any more.

It's one in the morning, and I'm lying in the dark, the curtains open wide, the warm air moving over my skin. I can't sleep, because of the heat and a homesickness which I'm used to, which has nothing to do with being away from my flat in London. I think of the sea, and the noise of the waves. When I first moved to the city, it took me a while to realize what I was listening for all the time. In London, if I'm half-asleep, I make distant traffic on the flyover into the snarl of a winter sea. I wish I could hear the river, but it slides silently through the fields, hidden. The current runs deep and strong.

'Neen. Neen.'

'Come in.'

I pull the sheet over me and sit up. Isabel pushes the door open, and comes in.

'Put the light on.'

She crosses the floor and switches on the little lamp by the bed.

'I didn't wake you up, did I?'

'No. I was listening for the river.'

'You can't hear it.'

'I know.'

Isabel goes to the window, and looks out. 'You can't even see it from here,' she says. 'Do you remember how we used to go out at night, without them knowing?'

'Yes.'

'You used to be frightened of how loud the sea sounded in the dark.' She yawns, pushes back her hair, rubs the stains of tiredness under her eyes.

'You should be asleep,' I say.

'He'll wake in less than an hour. It's hardly worth it.'

'You ought to let Susan give him a bottle at night so you can get some sleep. She said she would.'

'You bet she would. But she's not going to.' Isabel grins. 'Let her have her own baby.'

She comes back and sits on my bed. 'You know, *you* could feed him, Neen,' she says. 'Did you know that? Women who've never had babies can breastfeed if they keep on letting the baby suck. Some women strap little pouches of milk to themselves when they adopt a baby, with a tube running to their nipple, so he keeps sucking till the real milk comes.' She looks at me, smiling, and her hair shines with wisps of light.

'He's not my baby,' I say.

'Don't get cross. It's just a piece of information.'

The baby is everything. Everything starts in him and circles back to him, and the rest of us are shadows on the outside of the circle. Me, Richard, Susan. I wonder how Richard feels about it.

'You think I put him first,' says Isabel.

'It's natural,' I say, coolly, lightly. Or so I hope. I feel as if Isabel has just snatched her hand out of mine.

'That's a laugh,' says Isabel. 'I'll tell you something, Neen. When it was happening, when I started bleeding and I saw the midwife's face and then Richard was running to the phone, all I thought was, "Don't let me die." I didn't think of the baby. I thought of me. I thought I was going to bleed to death.'

'You nearly did.'

'I know.' She plucks at the ragged end of the bedspread, and then asks abruptly, 'Neen, do you think about death a lot?'

'Sometimes.'

'Richard says he never does.'

'He's probably lying.'

'But aren't people different? Isn't it frightening, how different they are?'

She looks at me intently, and yet I have the feeling she's still holding back from me. Then she says suddenly, 'Does Richard talk to you?'

I feel myself blush, for no reason, but I answer easily, 'Not much. You know he never does.'

'No.' I'm not sure if her face relaxes slightly, or not. 'Maybe he will, while you're here. After all, you're my sister. If he can't talk to you, who can he talk to? It'd do him good.'

Suddenly I remember something Isabel must have forgotten. A picnic, when I was sixteen. A cool windy afternoon and we walked above the railway line to Carbis Bay. Michael was with us, Isabel's friend from London. I was drawing two fishing-boats as they wallowed round the point. I had my back to Michael and Isabel, and I'd almost forgotten them, when Isabel said in a high, insistent voice, 'You could draw him, couldn't you, Neen? You could draw Michael?'

I didn't want to. I didn't want to break off what I was doing. But they were older, and they wanted something from me, and I rarely felt that Isabel wanted anything I had to give. I began to draw him, sitting against a stone way-marker. He was good-looking in a way Isabel liked then, thin and a bit evasive-looking. The wind tugged at his hair and my paper, but he was easy to draw and I knew it was coming out well. He got up once to look at what I'd done so far, and after that he suddenly became much more interested and began to talk to me, asking me about my drawing and what I was going to do when I left home. I saw why Isabel liked him once his face was lit up with flattering attention and it was all flowing my way. The drawing went better and better. We were talking about him now, the film he wanted to make, the famous actor who had more or less promised to be in it. Isabel had wandered off somewhere. When she came back the sun was out on the sheltered spot where I was drawing, and I'd nearly finished. Michael called to her, 'Have a look at this! You should have told me she was really good.' Isabel stooped, smiling, and examined what I'd done. Then she looked measuringly at Michael, a long look.

The next day Michael went home, three days early. I thought he'd have taken the drawing, since he'd asked me if he could have it, but he didn't. I found it crumpled on top of the kitchen rubbish, where he must have thrown it.

'You will stay, won't you?' asks Isabel. It seems to echo, as if she's asked the question before.

'I said I'd stay as long as you needed me,' I say. 'But you're all right, with Susan and Richard, and Edward. I'm not doing much except the cooking. You don't really need me here.'

Isabel frowns. The rich, half-hooped upper eyelids drop over her eyes as she looks down. Her long fingers pluck, pluck at the bedclothes. They are thin, and her wrists are oblong, showing their bones. Only her breasts are heavy. 'I do need you,' she says, not looking at me.

Chapter Eight

I told Susan that there were just the two of us, Isabel, and me, and this is what I always say. But there were three.

My brother was born when I was four years old. Like Isabel earlier, when I was born, I was old enough to notice my mother's pregnancy. It seemed endless. For years, it seemed, she ported a hump in front of her, big and tense and white when she was undressed. Her belly button turned inside out, like a mushroom stalk. I touched it, and she jumped and pushed me away. Every afternoon she locked the studio door, went upstairs to her bedroom and lay down. We were not allowed to make a noise then, or go to her unless one of us hurt ourselves. It was a late pregnancy: my mother was forty-three and hadn't expected to have another child. I don't know whether she wanted it or not, while she was pregnant, because everything is coloured afterwards by the real presence of the child.

I didn't want it. She was my mother, mine and Isabel's. Why had she chosen to make things worse like this? There wasn't enough money for us two, let alone a baby. That was why our father was away more and more. I knew this because Isabel listened to them talking, and told me.

'What's it like, having a baby?' I asked Isabel, and she wrinkled her nose, remembering. 'Noisy,' she said at last. We'd both been born in the house, but this time my mother was going to hospital, because she was older. There were streaks on my mother's stomach now, red and purple as it stretched. I don't remember my father much from that time.

The day the baby was born was fine and hot. Isabel was given a picnic, a pound note and two boxes of Rowntrees Fruit Gums, and told to take me to the beach for the day. We walked round beyond the surfing beach to a little cove of white sand we knew, where we could make a house by draping seaweed over the black rocks, and stick our lemonade bottle in cold sand.

'She'll be pushing it out now,' said Isabel, who knew everything about babies. I nodded, humping the canvas picnic bag over my shoulder while she shook a stone out of her sandal. I didn't care about the baby that day, because Isabel was going to let me fish off the rocks with her fishing-line for the first time.

Isabel held me tight round the waist as the waves sucked below us. The water was deep here, and dangerous. If we fell in we knew we'd be battered against the rocks. We were far out, too far out. My face was sticky with spray and every time I opened my mouth I tasted salt. The tide was on the turn, surging past our feet. Isabel's hands held me tight as I leaned out to throw the line clear of the rocks, and then we sat back in our niche of rock to wait for the tug. A hundred yards away, on safe rock, a man waved his arms at us. His mouth opened and closed but we couldn't hear anything above the noise of the waves.

'Stupid idiot,' said Isabel. 'Still, we'd better go back and see if she's had the baby yet.'

I don't remember the journey back, only my father, his face suddenly smooth with happiness, telling us it was a boy. He said it over and over, and Isabel and I looked at each other, a quick, furtive look. Then Isabel said, 'Oh, a boy. Never mind, Neen,' and she kneeled down and put her arms round me, mouthing over my head to our father, 'Neen wanted it to be a girl.' I'd wanted nothing, but I hid my face in Isabel's shirt because it was nice to feel her holding me. After a while my father said that he was going to the hospital, and he went.

They called the baby Colin. I thought about him a lot for the first day, and then forgot him. My mother was in hospital for ten days, and that was what I mostly thought about. Isabel put me to bed each night while our father visited the hospital. There must have been other adults around, friends and neighbours, but I only remember Isabel sitting on the linen chest by the bath squeezing shampoo on to my hair and then rubbing it in.

When my mother came back, she had Colin with her. He seemed to be stuck to her all the time so that whenever I wanted to climb into her lap he was there. She bottle-fed him, because she wanted to get back to work in the studio as soon as possible, and a girl was going to come in every day to look after him. But he fed and screamed, fed and screamed. Once she upset the hot water in which the feeding-bottle stood, and it ran over his foot so he screamed more. But when he stopped feeding she lifted him up and held his face against hers. She shut her eyes and whispered things to him which I couldn't hear.

She was tired for a long time, and not well. I remember creeping in very quietly and lying down beside her on the big double bed while she slept. She opened her eyes and saw me and smiled. Then Colin screamed.

'You ought to smack him, then he wouldn't make so much noise,' I told her. But she toiled out of bed and heated his milk.

Colin was three months old. Once I heard my parents talking about Isabel. 'It's strange that she doesn't bother with him, when you think how wonderful she is with Neen.'

Isabel never asked to hold Colin. Sometimes our mother would say, 'Here you are, would you like to hold him?' Isabel would let him loll in her lap until he was taken away. Afterwards she would hoist me up into her lap, and tell me stories, because she could read and I couldn't. I leaned against her, talking in the baby language we spoke to our dolls. We tended Rosina and Mandy more than ever, rocking them, soothing them, dressing and undressing them. If Colin was in the room we wouldn't even glance at him.

One evening, after we'd gone to bed, we began a game of babies. Isabel took the sheet and laid me in the middle of it, and then wrapped it round me tightly, like a shawl. At first I liked it and lay there sucking my thumb and smiling at her, talking baby-talk round the thumb. But then that got boring. I began to struggle free of the sheet. I was on my hands and knees, then on my feet in the deep trough in the middle of the bed.

'Naughty baby!' shouted Isabel, laughing, egging me on. I began to jump, bouncing on the mattress until the springs twanged. I jumped and jumped, screaming with excitement at every bounce. Isabel began to jump too, making me bounce twice, once on my jump and once on hers, while her long hair flew round us both. Suddenly the door opened. My mother was at the bed almost before we'd seen her. She grabbed my arm, and Isabel's.

'Shut up!' she shouted. 'Shut up! SHUT UP! You've woken him again and I'd just got him to sleep.'

Her face glared at us, white and frayed. She looked as if she'd like to kill us. I shrank towards Isabel. Suddenly my mother turned and went out of the room. I think she was afraid of starting to hit us and not being able to stop. We stood silent, listening to Colin's thin, rising howl. Isabel's cheeks were still red with jumping. I began to cry.

'Ssh, Neen!' she said. 'Don't make a noise or she'll come back.'

She got the sheet and wrapped me up in it again. This time I lay passive, staring up at her while she patted me to sleep, the way we patted our dolls.

When I woke up it was morning. Strong light was falling through the half-open curtains on to the lino, where Isabel sat cross-legged, reading a book. I wriggled the sheet loose, and rolled over. The house was still and quiet, full of sunlight, and Isabel looked up at me, turned down the corner of her page and smiled.

We must have played for an hour or so. Not dolls this time. I drew pictures, and Isabel made up stories about them. It must have been very early, in spite of the sun, because the house stayed quiet and the baby didn't cry. Suddenly Isabel said, 'I'm going to see Colin.' I stared at her in surprise, because neither of us ever went in to see Colin in the mornings. Even if we'd wanted to, we knew we mustn't ever wake him up. I remember I had a purple wax crayon in my fist. Isabel opened our door and went out, and I began to draw again. But straight away, she was back. She knelt down opposite me, poked her face close to mine, and announced. 'I don't think Colin's very well. You'd better come and have a look, Neen.'

She took my hand and led me out on to the landing. Colin slept in the tiny room over the stairs, and his door was open. Isabel pushed me in ahead of her, and I looked through the bars of his cot. But there was no Colin there. Instead there was a strange thing. I put my arm through the cot bar and felt it, and it was solid and cool, like my wax crayon. I looked at Isabel.

'Where's our baby?'

She pointed into the cot. 'That's Colin. He's just gone a funny colour.'

'Oh,' I said. I looked again and saw that she was right.

'We'd better go and get dressed,' said Isabel, and we went out, closing the door carefully behind us, and back into our bedroom. We didn't make much noise, but something must have woken our mother, because a few minutes later we heard her padding along to the bathroom. After she'd pulled the chain she went to Colin's room, and a second later we heard her begin to scream.

That was my brother, who died of cot-death when he was three months old. Suddenly I wonder if Richard even knows that there was ever such a person.

Chapter Nine

Alex came down with a salmon yesterday. He'd driven through the night when the motorways were almost empty, with the salmon lying on the back seat. It was hot in the car at midnight, he said. He had music on and the windows open as if he was driving in another country, not here. He didn't stay long. He talked to Edward for an hour in Isabel's room, and then he ate bread and cheese in the kitchen and drove away again. But Edward looks happier, and the salmon was left for us. Alex caught it himself. He's on holiday in Scotland, alone, fishing. The fish kept him company on the way down, wrapped in a freezer pack, and now Alex has gone back the five hundred miles, driving back to the rowan trees and the heather, which is just beginning to flush with colour. He looked round Isabel's garden as if it wasn't real, and his car keys kept jingling in his hand. He was elsewhere in his mind. I've always liked Alex, and I liked him even more when I saw him come in carrying the salmon like a baby.

Today I'm going to cook. We'll eat together, in the dark, cool dining-room. I'm going to bake the salmon, very slowly, with dill and juniper berries. I'll serve it just warm, with hollandaise sauce, with new potatoes, French beans, a big ripe cucumber which tastes of fruit, not water, and plum tomatoes from Isabel's greenhouse. They're so ripe that they're splitting at the stalk. And then an apple tart and a gooseberry fool. It'll take most of the day, especially on Isabel's cooker. We'll eat at seven, when the baby's been fed and bathed and with luck will sleep for two hours, even three. Richard is in London today, being interviewed by a financial journalist, but he'll be back at five.

This morning I took the fish out of the freezer and un-wrapped it. It was a big, lithe, silvery creature, hardly a scale on it damaged. Alex had packed it carefully, with a sprig of heather in its mouth. He had gutted it, and the flaps of its belly lay neatly together, like lips. It would be sweeter in flavour, more intense, less fatty than a farmed animal. He had wiped the blood off it. It lay on its long dish arched a little, as if remembering a leap.

Edward came in as I was spreading a piece of foil loosely over the fish to keep the flies off while it thawed. It should have been muslin, because foil can rub off the scales, but I hadn't thought to buy any when I went shopping early that morning.

'Is that for tonight?' he asked, and I nodded.

'Do you want a hand?'

I looked up, thinking quickly. I never give away the jobs I like best, I'm not that sort of cook.

'You can get the dining-room ready. Polish the table and dust the chairs. That'll save me a lot of time.'

'OK,' he said, surprising me again. 'Where's the stuff?'

I found rags for him, and a hardened lump of beeswax polish. Isabel has no dusters. The house is neither clean nor very dirty, and it reminds me of how things were when we were little, with sand choking the wash-basin, shells and seaweed behind the kitchen sink, too much rubbish in the tiny bin which my mother lined with newspaper, and dead bluebottles lying for weeks on window-ledges until they seemed like friends. Sometimes Isabel pours Jeyes Fluid down her drains, or boiling water on to an ants' nest which is too near the kitchen, as our mother did. When I watch Isabel do these things I am at home, as if something is going on which is beyond liking, beyond even love. There's a way that my mother would lift the corner of a sheet or a blouse to her face and sniff it for damp after she'd brought in the washing. I've made myself stop doing this, but Isabel goes on. She lines her compost bin with newspaper, too, so that the parcel of peelings and eggshells falls apart soggily when I lift it out.

I am smiling, and Edward is looking at me, ready to smile too.

The tart will take longest. I've bought white Normandy butter, pastry flour, three pounds of sharp, sweet Jonagold apples. They are not the right apples, but I won't get better in the fag-end of the season, before the new apples come in. They must be cut evenly, in fine crescents of equal thickness which will lap round in ring after ring, hooping inwards, glazed with apricot jam. The tart must cook until the tips of the apple rings are almost black, but the fruit itself is still plump and moist. When you close your eyes and bite you must taste caramel, sharp apple, juice and the short, sandy texture of sweet pastry all at once. No one taste should be stronger than another. The pastry is made, and resting in the fridge. One piece of equipment which Isabel does possess, among her rusty whisks and wooden spoons which smell of onion, is a huge marble slab with a broken edge. I made the pastry on it, cutting the butter into the heaped flour and rubbing it in quickly, lightly, so the paste just held together.

I'm simmering the reduction for the hollandaise sauce. It smells of bay leaf, more than I think it should. I wonder if I should add a second slice of onion, and then decide not to. It bubbles and thickens, releasing the spiciness of mace and a sharp vinegar smell. I love making sauces, real sauces which glisten with egg-yolks and lump after lump of butter. I strain the reduction, thin it slightly and begin to whisk in the egg-yolks. Now for the stage I like best. I've got a pan of water simmering on a ring, but it's still too high, the water bubbling with more energy than it needs. The controls on these rings are crude. I turn it down and the water seems to go to sleep. Up, and it bubbles. I fiddle again, and at last I get what I want. The water squirms, almost unnoticeably alive. I place my bowl of sauce over it and put in the first lump of butter, watch it start to slither, and then whisk. I drop in another lump, whisk again, and go on, watching it thicken, checking the heat, making sure the sauce stays smooth as ointment and doesn't curdle. There are twelve lumps of butter to go in. The sauce swallows them all, gleaming, fattening on what I've given it. I let it cook a little longer, still whisking gently. Now it looks right. I dip in a clean wooden spoon and the sauce coats it perfectly.

The last bit is easy. Lemon juice, a touch of salt and pepper. I dip in the wooden spoon again, run my finger over its back, then taste, closing my eyes.

'I bet that's good,' says Richard behind me.

I turn and hold out the spoon. 'Have some if you want. You're back early.'

'It didn't take as long as I thought.'

'Did it go all right?'

'Fine. It'll be in next Thursday's *FT*.'

He's pleased with himself, the man who's been somewhere and done something. He smells of trains. He looks at the fish, ready to cook now, wrapped in its shroud of buttered foil.

'What's that? Alex's salmon?'

'Yes.'

He hovers, smiling, and I put the sauce to one side. 'It's time to put it in,' I say, and lift the salmon. Richard kneels and opens the oven door.

'It's not very hot,' he says.

'It doesn't need to be.'

The salmon just fits. I have already checked, so I'm not surprised when it slides in by a whisker. The salmon is in the oven, the potatoes ready to boil, the tomatoes in a warm heap on the table, to be cut as late as possible and sprinkled with chopped basil and brown sugar. The beans are waiting in a colander. The tomatoes are intensely red against the damaged surface of the table. Their skins are tough. I'll score them with the point of a knife, dip them in boiling water and slip them out of their skins.

Richard has left the outside door open and a bright tongue of sunlight lies on the stone floor. I think of flowers on the table, of a last-minute picking of warm gooseberries and crushing them with a fork, of the cream I've already whipped to fold into them. I think of our seven bodies, mine, Richard's, Isabel's, the baby's, Alex's, Susan's, Edward's. Alex will be back by his river, a halo of flies round his head. The heat is thinner up there, burning the bracken brown and the rowan berries first to orange, then deep red. The waters he fishes are so sweet that when he's thirsty he cups his hands, dips them and drinks. Isabel is sitting in the rocking-chair, rocking back and forward, back and forward, her eyes half-open. The baby is with Susan, visiting her mother. Susan's tied him into a sling and walked him across the fields for tea, his little bare head covered in a denim sun-hat. Edward has polished the table and laid it for five, and now he's typing a long letter to Alex into his lap-top. But it's too hot to think and his fingers slip on the keys. A small plane has gone over twice, with a long streamer dragging behind it which says 'Visit Damiano's Dreamworld'.

And Richard's here. 'Do you want a drink?' he asks. I look through the window and suddenly the shadows seem bluer, looser. The endless afternoon is nearly over.

They're all sitting down, waiting, even Isabel. I can hear them from the kitchen: a laugh, then a murmur, like the sound of an audience settling in its seats. Everything is on the table now except the salmon. It's been out of the oven for half an hour, resting and cooling inside its foil. I take a pair of scissors and cut a corner of foil, run the line of the blade along it, then fold it back from the fish. I smear my two hands with butter and ease them under the salmon, and then lift. It comes up perfectly, its bright silvery skin intact, and I lay it down again on a bed of fresh dill, on a clean white plate. I wash my hands.

When I bring it in Isabel begins to clap, lightly, her hands level with her eyes so that I can't see them. Edward claps too, his face set in the little ironic smile which is like a tic with him. Richard does not clap. As I put down the heavy dish I see him swallow the saliva that has gathered in his mouth.

'Ooh!' says Susan. 'Isn't it beautiful? It seems a shame to eat it.'

But we eat it. Its flesh falls from the bones, the colour of coral. Its spine shows like a ruined nave. Its eyes have sunk in cooking and they look inward, filmed like an old man's eyes. Tatters of skin and scale hang from the bones as we eat on, filling and refilling our plates, each mouthful of fish dipped in the sauce, which is not golden at all in this light, but pale as primroses. The salmon's flesh is creamy, with a faint, fresh tang of the sea.

'You can't buy salmon like this,' says Richard. 'It's a shame Alex didn't stay to eat it.'

Isabel puts out her hand and touches Edward's sleeve. 'You'll be going up there yourself next week, won't you?' she says. 'You'll be eating salmon every night.'

'Until you're sick of it, like a London apprentice,' says Richard, and lifts his glass again, and drinks. He's drunk a lot already. Isabel looks at him, a slight frown stitching itself on to her forehead. Of course, I realize suddenly, Isabel's sober. She can't drink because she's feeding the baby. That's why she has that removed, censorious look.

I'm far from sober. As soon as the salmon landed on the table I began to drink. My day of kitchen power was over. Let them stub out cigarettes in the bones of the salmon if they wanted.

The tart is finished and waiting, the cream whipped. The gooseberry fool is chilling. I need do nothing but eat and drink. I drank the first couple of glasses quickly, straight off, on an almost empty stomach, and instantly the room glowed and swam. Now, drinking the third, I remember the wine I had earlier, with Richard. I feel myself raised up as the blue shine of evening strokes the long table, the wrecked and polished skin of the salmon. There are swifts jinking outside the window, and swallows going home to their nests under the barn eaves. I think of owls, fucking the wind. My body goes soft with the thought of it.

Susan has pushed her hair back behind a dark band, so that she looks like a squash player. Her mouth gleams with butter, and her hands cut the food up very small, so it is almost unrecognizable, before she eats it. From time to time she darts a quick look at one face or another. Isabel has stopped eating, though her plate is almost full. She has an unlit cigarette between her fingers, but she seems to have forgotten about it. Richard gets up and moves clumsily past me, on his way to the kitchen for bread. He always wipes his plate with bread. He staggers and puts his hand down hard on my shoulder, for balance.

'Bring in the tart,' I say. Susan laughs loudly, and sprays potato through her teeth. Edward turns and scrubs at her with a napkin, like an elder brother, while Isabel leans forward and lights her cigarette from one of the candles, which are suddenly bright, because when I haven't been noticing it, it's gone dark.

Time which I don't notice passes. Richard bangs the tart down on the table in front of me, so hard that I think the crust must have broken. But it hasn't. Usually I can't bear anyone but me to cut into a pie or tart I've made, but tonight I can't be bothered. 'Help yourselves. It might as well be eaten,' I say, as if the food's nothing. I stare at the apples running rings round the dish. Isabel shakes her head, a tiny shake, and draws on her cigarette. Susan hesitates, looks round again before taking the offered dish and plunging in the knife. She cuts herself a small piece.

'Cut a big piece,' says Edward. 'You know you want to.' Susan giggles, and cuts again. 'I'll pour the cream for you,' adds Edward, and lifts the jug high.

'Let her do it for herself,' says Isabel quietly. Edward glances at her, and puts the jug into Susan's hand.

Richard has filled my glass. I drink off the yellowish wine without bothering to taste it much, though it's good. I take the bottle and fill my empty glass again, right to the top. I am quite drunk, and I want to be much drunker.

'I want to see the owls,' I hear myself say suddenly.

'I can show you them if you want. They're nesting in our barn,' says Susan.

'Let's all go,' says Richard.

'They won't be there now.' Isabel stubs out her cigarette. 'It's night time. They'll be hunting.' Then she tenses. 'Was that him?' she asks.

'I don't think so,' says Susan, spooning cream.

'I'm sure it was.' Isabel rises. She's wearing a dress I haven't seen before, a silk dress, long and slim. It's a deep, blackish red, the colour of ripe mulberries. Automatically I look down at what I'm wearing. Black trousers, a cream linen shirt. I wonder if I'll ever not feel this pang, so deep it seems to have been put in there by nature.

'I might as well feed him in bed,' says Isabel.

'Are you going to bed?' asks Richard. 'It's early.'

'Not for me. Come in quietly, or you'll wake him up when I've just got him off. Or you could sleep down here, on the sofa. That might be easier.'

She looks at him and he looks at her, swivelling with that blind, baited look I've seen on him before.

'All right,' he says.

Chapter Ten

I stumble on the stairs and bang my shin hard. It seems safest to crawl up the last few stairs and on to the landing, where there's a strip of light under Isabel's door.

'Isabel?'

The door opens and there's Isabel with the baby slung over her shoulder.

'What are you doing down there?'

'I've got to sit down, Iz, I feel awful.'

'I thought you were drinking a lot.'

I sprawl in Isabel's armchair and watch her sit down again, patting the baby's back. The room is too bright, so I shut my eyes.

'I suppose Richard's still boozing.'

'He's gone out for a walk with Edward and Susan.'

'You should have gone too.'

I make a huge effort and open my eyes. 'No I shouldn't. Better here.'

'I wonder if it's colic. He's all right as long as I do this, but as soon as I put him down he starts screaming.'

Isabel stands up and begins to walk the baby up and down, up and down the same strip of floor.

'I can remember doing this with you,' she says.

'You can't, can you?'

'I used to put you in the doll's pram and take you for walks. I remember how people used to look in thinking I had a doll in there, and then they'd see it was a real baby. You should have seen their faces. I used to have you all tucked in and parade you up and down the street. Then I'd take you down the hill, holding on tight to the handrail in case the pram ran away with me. It nearly did, lots of times. Everyone used to say I was a proper little mother. I used to think I was the bee's knees. God knows what they thought really.'

I watch her walking, her right hand patting Antony's tiny humped back.

'You didn't eat the meal I made,' I say suddenly.

'It was wonderful, Neen. Everyone said it was wonderful. But you know I can't eat meals like that.'

She looks at me steadily, over the baby's head. I have never heard Isabel admit as much as this before, though I know it, of course I know it. I've just chosen to pretend that things change and people alter, and Isabel makes it easy for people to pretend. She's always had her breakfast early, she's always going to eat her lunch in the garden, or else she doesn't feel like supper yet. The fact is that Isabel can't eat round a table with other people. When I look back I can't remember whether she ever could or not. Our mother would leave sandwiches and apples for her under covered plates, and let her go into the larder to fetch what she wanted when she wanted it. I raged because it was so unfair, but for once my mother was immovable.

'Why can't I have Rice Krispies for tea like Isabel?'

'Isabel's different.'

I wonder how she's managing. Our mother was always worried that Isabel didn't eat enough, but no one was allowed to say a word to Isabel about food.

'But you're feeding him. Aren't you hungry?'

Isabel points to her bedside table.

'Look in the drawer.'

'I don't think I can get up.'

'Yes, you can.'

The table lurches, faraway then close. I snatch at the knob and the drawer slides open.

'There you are,' says Isabel, 'oatcakes and dried apricots. I eat them all the time, and they're full of iron. So you don't need to worry.'

I think of the house filling up with the smells of food all day, and Isabel sitting here, eating an apricot, a quarter of oatcake. Perhaps she did say more about it once. I remember her voice saying something about people's mouths opening and closing, their hands reaching out for food, and all of it unreal and slowed down, as if time was stuck and she was stuck there too. She always hated people who ate too much, except me. She liked me to eat. Yes, now I do remember. There was a time when Isabel used to be able to eat in front of me, as if I was part of herself. But I don't know when it ended.

'I hope the baby won't be like me,' says Isabel. 'Do you think he will?'

I look at the baby, wheezily sleeping on Isabel's shoulder, limp as a rag. Its eyes are so tight shut there is only the thinnest line. 'He doesn't look very like you,' I say.

'I can't bear to think of what might happen to him,' says Isabel, her voice low and intense.

'Nothing's going to happen to him.'

'How do you know?' she asks. 'How can you tell? Anything could happen. Babies can't tell anybody anything, no matter what happens to them.'

'Nothing happened to me, though, did it? – and you were only four or five, pushing me all round town.'

'He's not like you,' says Isabel, so quietly I can hardly hear her. 'Look at him. Who do you think he looks like?'

I peer at the baby, but he looks like no one to me. 'He's a bit like Dad, isn't he?' I suggest, because someone else has already said it.

'Yes, I suppose so.' The tension has gone out of her voice. 'Yes, I suppose he is quite like Dad when you come to look at him.'

I'm lying flat on my back on Isabel's bed, without knowing how I got there.

'Don't go to sleep, Neen.' I jump. The tension is back in her voice.

'What's matter?'

'Does the baby look all right to you?'

I prop myself up and inspect the small, shut face. He's the same colour as he was earlier, and he seems to be breathing.

'Izzy, of course he's all right. You're just tired. I'll go, then you can get some sleep.'

'Don't go, Neen.'

'But you've got to rest.' And the drink's abandoning me, leaving vast fatigue like mud in an estuary when the tide's gone out. I drag myself off the bed.

'Go and find Edward then. Tell him I need him.'

'But Izzy, he'll have gone to bed.'

'He won't. He won't mind.'

'OK then. Sure you don't want me to stay?'

'It's all right. Get Edward.'

I find Edward in the kitchen. We didn't touch the gooseberry fool earlier, but Edward's found it. He sits at the kitchen table with one arm curled round the bowl, digging into it. He raises his spoon in salute.

'Delicious. You really are an excellent cook, Nina.'

'Isabel wants you.' My tongue feels too big for my mouth, too big for any explanations with Edward. He seems to go at once or, at least, not to be there when I next look. And someone's done the washing-up. I walk back through the dining-room, where the table shines, empty. The candles are out, stiff with congealed wax, and the flowers stand in a pool of dropped petals. In the next room, the sitting-room, I find Richard asleep on the sofa, face down, his head hidden in his arms. He's snoring. On the other side of the room there's Susan, sitting on a cushion under the window.

'Oh good,' she says, 'here you are. Don't worry, he's all right. I've put him in the recovery position.'

'What?'

'The recovery position. He'll be perfectly safe.'

'What's happened? Did he have an accident?'

'He was terribly drunk,' mouths Susan, as if Richard might hear us. 'You know there's always a risk of inhaling vomit.'

'Good God.' I stare at Richard. 'You mean you put him lying like that.'

Susan smiles proudly. 'They taught us how to lift on the course,' she says. 'He's a big man, but it wasn't too tricky. Edward couldn't help because he's got a bad back.'

'Oh, well. Well done,' I say. Susan's eyes shine. She looks like an angel in this light, with her fair hair turned white, standing up round her head and held back by the black band. She brims with questions, her mouth already opening to ask how Isabel is, why Richard's drunk, what I'm going to do with the leftover salmon. But I point at Richard, put my finger on my lips, and back out of the room. It's quite time this evening was over.

I undress in the dark, leaving the curtains open. I wish I was in London now, with orange street glow coming in through the curtains I'm always meaning to replace with something thicker. I'd like to wake up to a dull day and the swish of tyres through rain. This country darkness makes my eyes ache as I try to peer through it. But it's not really dark now. The more I look, the more shadows I see. A soft yellow half-moon is caught in the branches of a tree. Then it breaks free and rises like a bubble of air from a diver. I pull on a navy T-shirt and sit on the bed and watch the sky.

But I must see Isabel. She wanted me to stay, and I didn't. I'm always wanting her to want me, and then when she does I'm out of the door. I'd rather listen to her telling me about when I was her baby. I'm her sister, and it was me she wanted, not Edward.

I don't knock. I push Isabel's door open gently, in case she's asleep. And there they are. Edward must have been sitting in the chair beside her bed for a long time. He holds one of Isabel's hands. His left foot is on the cradle rocker, rocking gently, rhythmically, as if he's treadling an old sewing-machine. The baby and Isabel are both asleep. She lies flat, sunk into the bed, her head on one side. The cradle is facing me, and I can see the baby's head, his fists up by the sides of his face. Edward has his back to the door, his head bowed, so I think at first that perhaps he's asleep too. But he's awake. He hears the door creak. Without letting go of Isabel's hand, or altering the gentle pressure on the cradle rocker, he turns his head and looks over his shoulder at me. He shakes his head, a tiny shake which does not disturb either Isabel or the baby at all. There's nothing to do but go away.

I think of the hours Edward spends in Isabel's room, talking about Alex, making Isabel pour out the oil of her understanding and advice on him. And giving nothing back. Why does she do it? Why does she have them here, Edward and Alex and all the others who come for supper and stay a week? Exhausting her, draining her, keeping her from what she really wants to do. I can never see her alone.

That's how I've always seen it. I suppose everyone has a story about the people they love, and that's been mine about Isabel. It's a safe story, well-worn and comforting. One of those stories children get addicted to, asking for them again and again and pushing all the other books aside. Perhaps I tell myself this story so loudly that I can't hear anything else. Otherwise why would she lie there, sunk in sleep, leaving her baby to Edward? And that look he gave me, as if I'd met his expectation exactly. He knows more about me than I thought.

Chapter Eleven

I fall into sleep hungrily, as if it's food, and dreams crowd in. It's because I'm not working. I always dream too much when I'm not working, because all the images I ought to be making lie in wait until I sleep.

I dream of a garden which is Isabel's, but different. The grass in Isabel's garden is burned to the colour of a camel by the hot summer, but this grass is soft and green. I'm beside a long border of flowers, backed by a thick yew hedge. The black-green hedge is starred with out-of-season berries, like jam tarts. There are golden rod and rudbeckia in flower, burning yellow. And there's an overwhelming smell of catnip. I look along and see that the whole border is edged with it. There are small apple trees growing among the flowers, heavy with ripe apples, so heavy that some of the branches have broken and the white, torn wood shows.

Someone's coming. I'm thinking of Isabel, but it isn't Isabel I'm waiting for. I'm alive with excitement. I look down and see I'm wearing a dress I've never seen before. I feel beautiful and on edge. I'm wearing this dress because I'm going to meet someone, here, now. The name won't come, but it's someone I know well. There are bees all over the border, in the catnip and clinging to the heads of the golden rod, bending them down with a weight of bee bodies. I start to walk up and down, up and down, feeling my skirt move against my legs.

In the second dream nothing happens. It's a dream about the river, wider and deeper than it is now after weeks of drought. The water's a different colour too, like brown glass. I'm standing on the bank looking down. There are tiny pebbles at the bottom, as clear as if they were in my hand, and lodged among them there's a very small plastic doll, a doll's house doll, naked, with wide eyes. The water sways over them and someone says behind me: 'Those pebbles are boulders. It's only the depth that makes them look so small.'

I try to move back, terrified now that I see how deep this water is, but the same voice says, 'Careful. Stay where you are. If you move you'll fall in.'

'Fax for you.' Richard hands it to me and I read it eagerly, glad of proof that I've got a life outside this house. I read it again to be sure I've got it right. Yes. The Cruzet Foundation is going to use me on the Music House recording visits. It means three trips to Romania, two weeks each. They want a different kind of record, sketches as well as photographs. That's why I've got it, because there'll have been a lot of photographers in the running who have more experience than me. I spent a couple of days with a music therapist getting a cameo project folder together and working out the basis of my proposal. At the time it seemed stupid – a whole two days which I'd never be able to cost into my fee. But you have to be stupid sometimes, to get into the kind of work you really want.

'You look pleased.'

'I never thought I'd get it. It's a terrific piece of work.'

'I read the fax,' says Richard, 'but I couldn't make much sense of it. What's the Music House?'

'It's an orphanage in Romania.'

'Jesus. You're not going to one of those places, are you?'

'What did you see, when I said an orphanage in Romania?'

'I don't know. Newspaper pictures. Kids with shaved heads and big eyes and brain damage. But they're not in the papers any more, are they? They've had their five minutes.'

'That's what this project's about, about it not having to be like that. The house uses music in everything, so even the kids who can't speak all play in the house band and learn to sing. They choose a piece of music which becomes theirs, like another name. Some of them lost their names, because they were abandoned when they were too young to know them. They each get given an instrument as soon as they come and no one else is allowed to touch it. They'll smash it up but it's always replaced. When they started most of the instruments were home-made, but now they've been given a lot of stuff and they have a concert every night after they've eaten. There are two music therapists working out there now, as well as this woman who began it. She still works with the children twelve hours a day. Can you imagine what I'll be able to do, living there for two weeks at a time?'

'I can see why you got the job. You've certainly done the homework,' says Richard.

'But it really is unique. No one else has tried anything like it.'

'I'm not saying it's not.'

I pick up my mug of coffee and drink. I'm longing to look through the fax again but I'll hold back while Richard's here, since he's clearly not that interested. A green little do-gooder, that's what he makes me feel like. But bugger him. He doesn't see what I want. The children separate as droplets, the instruments talking to each other long before the children are able to do so. Groups of children playing together, a single face coming into light and then reabsorbed into shadow. I can see splinters of light, splinters of sound. I'll use a camcorder too, and then freeze the images and draw from them. I can see myself collaging, drawing across the grain of the prints. In a way it won't matter what the facilities are like, how rough it is. That's what I want. Rough, immediate, tense work. Like a steel band, but with moments of hush that take your breath away.

'I must fax back. Is that OK?'

'Of course. Use it any time, and the computer if you like. I was wondering how you were keeping up with your work.'

'I've only been here eight days, and I haven't taken a holiday since Christmas.'

'Is it only eight days? It seems longer.'

'Thanks.'

'I didn't mean that,' he says. 'I didn't mean that, Nina, and you've got me wrong about this Romanian thing too. I admire you.'

I flush deeply and turn away, fumbling with the kettle switch. Patter repeats in my head, the patter that I gave Richard, the patter on paper that got me the job. I push in the switch and the kettle hisses dryly.

'I'm very good at boiling up an empty kettle,' I tell him.

'Aren't we all.'

He is pouched, heavy, shadowed by hangover. He's washed thoroughly in some sharp-smelling soap, and put on a clean white shirt. I recognize the impulse: I've washed my own hair and it's still wet.

'The sun's getting hot. You could sit outside and dry your hair.'

'I thought I'd go in and see Isabel.'

'She's talking to Edward.'

There's no clue to what he thinks or feels. 'Let's walk round the garden,' he says. 'It might clear my head.'

The paths keep narrowing so there is not quite room for two people to walk abreast. I've never noticed this before now but it's awkward, almost ridiculous. One of us is always having to bob ahead, holding back a branch, or else we're apologizing for bumping into one another.

'Let's sit on this seat,' says Richard. It is full in the sun, and Isabel has put a terracotta pot full of golden marjoram beside us. The garden is full of early business, birds slashing at a near-ripe fig, bees fumbling in and out of flowers. We are quite hidden here.

'I think she's getting worse,' says Richard.

I say nothing, because I know he isn't talking about the healing of Isabel's wound.

'She hasn't been out in the garden since you came, has she?'

'She must have been.' But I think back. Has she?

'I think she tried, the first morning after I was back. Her shoes were wet. But she was back in bed looking awful by the time I woke up. I slept in the armchair.'

'She's been in a lot of pain.'

'I'm not talking about pain. I don't think she can go outside any more, do you understand what I mean?'

I understand what he means. It's the same as the food, it all seems so reasonable until you look closely. Isabel doesn't drive, and the buses are awkward. She doesn't visit people. Why trail to London or anywhere else when people can come here? All her city friends can't wait to get away into the country. They come to see her, and they come eagerly, Edward, Alex and a dozen more. When did she last come to London? I think back. Not since she was pregnant. Not all last summer.

'What about the shopping?' Suddenly, urgently, I want to think of Isabel biking down the track and a couple of miles along the road to the nearest post office, coming back with over-priced mayonnaise and clothes-pegs bouncing in her basket.

'I do it,' says Richard. 'The only time she's been down that track for months is when she went into hospital. The midwife came here for the antenatal stuff, because she was supposed to be having the baby at home.'

'But she was all right in the hospital.'

My statement falls into silence. Silence is dangerous. Two people, the sun falling, getting hotter and hotter on my bare arms and legs. My hair must be nearly dry now. There's the noise of bees, swinging near, veering away again. Farther off a light chink of metal on metal comes from the barn. The sound of other people at work only makes this bench more private.

Richard's face glistens with sweat. He ought to wear a hat. I feel what he feels: the drink, the headache, the hangover, that airy frightened feeling of guilt for things that didn't happen last night – the kind of feeling that makes me want to walk away from myself without making a sound –

We kiss. Not touching much, only our lips. It feels as if there's all the time in the world. He's hot under his shirt and all the things I forget each time flood back: the tiny movements at first, the kissing deeper and deeper, the thickness of flesh before you touch bone. I thought I'd finished with this greed for the beginnings of things, but it comes again, better than anything I've tried to put in its place. I lean into Richard's heaviness, wanting it to swallow me.

'I've only ever wanted her,' says Richard. It's perhaps thirty seconds since the time before we'd kissed. He's sitting upright, thighs spread, hands clasped, hanging between them.

'I know.' But I'm a meticulous noter of tenses. *Up till now*, this means. All I have to think about is what 'now' means.

'And you don't love me, you love Isabel,' he says, putting his hand over mine.

'I'm not talking about love,' I say, and look him full in the face, 'but we can have a good fuck and none the wiser.'

I watch how his eyes narrow to strips, and then widen. His hand tightens on mine. He's looking straight back at me now, and thinking of nothing else.

'I'm not like Isabel,' I say, 'I told you that before. I like food, and I like fucking.'

'How many men have you slept with?' asks Richard.

'Nineteen,' I say immediately.

'Nineteen? You're sure about that?'

'It could be twenty. Ask me again tomorrow.'

'We can't do it here.'

'I don't see why not.'

'Someone might see.'

64

'I don't think so.'

'I see,' says Richard. 'You like an element of risk.'

'There always is one anyway, so why pretend? This is as good as anywhere.'

It was as good as anywhere.

'You're not taking off all your clothes, are you?' said Richard.

'Why not? It's still fucking even if I leave my bra on, so why not let's do it properly?'

He looks at me and I see a splinter of hesitation swim in his eye, like a minnow.

'You're thinking about those nineteen men,' I say. 'Don't worry, it's safe.'

'I wasn't thinking of that, Nina.'

'Then you should have been. That's what things are like. But I haven't got AIDS and I won't get pregnant, so it's safe.'

I sit down on the seat again, naked. Whatever he does, I'm fine. I could sit here all day soaking up heat and light.

'Women look so different without their clothes on,' he says, his voice changing.

'Yes they do, don't they? How many are you thinking of? Nineteen is it – or twenty?'

He laughs, sits down beside me, his leg in jeans against my bare leg. The sun burns on us. Richard slides his hand under my breast and watches my nipple stiffen.

'What if Susan came past?'

'She'd think we were about to fuck.'

'This bench hasn't got a back,' he says. 'If I knew you better I could ask you to lie on your stomach across it so I could fuck you from behind. But it's an awkward position.'

'That's what you want?'

'It's what I've always wanted.'

'Then it's what we'll do.'

I have short hair so it doesn't get in my way, hanging down and trailing on the ground. The position is awkward and the bench would be rough if I hadn't spread Richard's white shirt carefully over it, and used his jeans to make a pillow under my stomach.

'It'll be better if we get down on the ground,' says Richard. The grass is short, crisp and prickling with drought. I get down on hands and knees and then let the weight of my body fall on to my forearms. There is a marigold at eye-level, so close I smell its peppery smell. The dry grass under me, the grainy heart of the marigold, the long, still exposure, are all one. I get into position, raising myself, and Richard's finger slides, parting the lips of my wet vulva.

'It looks nice,' he says. 'You're ready for me, aren't you? I can tell you're ready for me.'

He says it with pleasure, with relief, with gratitude, not as some men would say it. The hot sun falls on our wetness and sweat, and a blackbird works away at a grub it's found, less than four feet away. My body stretches, every membrane willing to let him in.

Chapter Twelve

We've rolled behind the bench, into the shadow. We're lying there, our skin separating as it cools, when I hear the back door click.

'Put your clothes on,' I murmur in Richard's ear. His slack face tightens.

We throw on clothes, listening for footsteps, but there aren't any. Then there's a second of standing still, out of breath, Richard looking at me as if there's something more to be said. I smile at him and run my fingers through my hair.

'You look just the same,' he says.

'Of course.'

He reaches forward, hooks his fingers in the sides of my shorts, and slowly pulls them down. Then he kneels and presses his face into my stomach. I look down on his messed-up, wiry dark hair, but I don't touch it.

'We'll do it again,' I say, 'but not now. Susan's just come out. I can hear her talking to the baby.'

I walk down the little twisting paths on my own, rubbing my fingers on lavender and purple sage. My thighs ache. The paths cross one another, winding between low hedges, so you can walk round the garden many times and never go the same way. Here's a rough patch of gooseberry bushes and blackberries. The gooseberries are finished, but some of the blackberries are ripe, bigger than wild blackberries, fat, shiny and already black, though it's much too early. The sun's forcing everything. I eat a handful, and then sit down on the rough grass so I'm level with the bramble tips feeling their way down to root. I take some things out of my pocket: cigarette papers, a tobacco pouch, a small packet wrapped in silver foil, some matches. I stick the papers together, tear off cardboard from the packet and roll it up, spread tobacco over the paper. I open the foil, light a match and singe a corner of the brown resin, and then crumble it over the tobacco. Then I roll up the joint and twist the end. I wait for a long time before I smoke it. I want to draw those bramble tips as they arch down, nosing their way into the earth, which is so hard that they'll never be able to root. I can hear voices in the distance, but I can't tell whose they are. I close my eyes and sit cross-legged, simmering in a little tent of heat.

I can't get Isabel's doll out of my mind. Yes, I did cut off her eyelashes, thinking they'd grow again. I can still recall the crispy feel of the lashes between the scissor blades. Again and again I wished I'd called my doll Rosina instead of Mandy. One day I began to call her Amelia, but Isabel wasn't having any of that.

'You can't change her name now. How would *you* like it if we all stopped calling you Nina and started calling you Lynn?'

Lynn was my enemy three doors down. I knew Isabel meant what she said, and if I kept on with Amelia she would take away my name as well.

'Let's have a christening,' Isabel said.

We'd never been to a christening. Isabel and I used to sit on the wall on Sundays in our bare feet to scorn the tidy church-going boys and girls as they came by. Once Isabel took me to a Methodist Sunday school, explaining to the lady there that I was very interested in Jesus and our mummy and daddy wouldn't let me find out about him. This went down well, and the next thing I was colouring a donkey while Isabel won the prize for telling a Bible story in her own words. But the prize was only a packet of Spangles.

'I'm sorry,' said Isabel, 'our mummy doesn't allow us to eat sweets because of our teeth,' and she hauled me off the brown carpet where I was starting on the donkey's tail, which I'd left till last.

'What a load of shit,' said Isabel as we skipped off up the hill.

The christening Isabel organized was much better than Sunday school. We collected all the flowers we could find, the candytuft and marigolds and daisies that grew in our hot, dry garden. Isabel filled the washing-up bowl with water, and spread a tablecloth out on the grass. Another tablecloth was going to go round the shoulders of the priest. I could see that Isabel was torn between the two roles of mother and priest, but she solved this by wheeling Rosina and Mandy 'to the door of the church', and then quickly wrapping herself in her robes while I stood in as mother, clutching the dolls. Isabel muttered words I couldn't hear properly, and sprinkled flowers on the dolls' upturned faces. Then she seized Rosina and plunged her into the water. A second later Rosina bounced up to the surface, water rolling off her plastic skin.

'Right, she's done,' said Isabel in her normal voice. Then she took Mandy. Mandy went down as Rosina had done, but unlike Rosina she stayed there, bubbles of air streaming up from her soused curls.

'Oh dear,' said Isabel, 'I'm afraid she's stuck. Don't worry, mother, I'll pull her out.'

But I saw her hands tensed, pushing Mandy down. 'She doesn't want to come up, I'm afraid,' said Isabel.

'Get her up! Get her up!' I screamed.

Isabel grunted, pushing and pulling at the same time. Suddenly Mandy shot out of the bowl on a wave of water on to the parched grass and lay there still, face down and sodden. Isabel rushed to her and knelt down, her tablecloth robe hiding Mandy from my sight. I stood rooted. Slowly, Isabel turned. Her face was wet with real tears.

'I'm sorry, mother, I'm so sorry. Your little baby has drowned.'

I shut my eyes so as not to see what Isabel was holding, and screamed and screamed. My screams rang in my head, red as the sun through my closed eyelids. As long as I kept screaming nothing else could happen. I heard a sash window bang up; then Isabel grabbed my shoulders, shaking me, shouting, 'She's all right! Look, she's sitting up! It's a miracle!'

But I could not stop screaming, though I opened my eyes and saw Mandy sitting rigidly on the grass, her eyes staring blindly ahead of her. Our mother came out of the back door, wiping clay from her hands. Isabel rushed to her.

'Nina's crying because Mandy fell in the washing-up bowl and she thinks she's dead. I keep telling her she isn't but she won't listen.'

My mother knelt on the grass beside me and put one arm round me, and I stopped screaming.

'Isabel, give Mandy to me.'

My mother took the doll, turned her over and patted her back. 'That's to get the water out of Mandy's lungs. Now I'm going to turn her over and give her the kiss of life. Watch.'

My mother put her lips over Mandy's face. Slowly, gently, she breathed out into Mandy's mouth. She turned aside, took another breath, and breathed into Mandy again. After a while she stopped and said. 'There. It's working. Her colour's coming back. She just had a shock, Nina. She wasn't really drowned.'

I took Mandy from my mother. She felt soft again, and warm from my mother's skin. Her eyes looked at me, smiling.

'She's all right now,' said my mother, 'Pour the rest of that water away, Isabel.'

Isabel poured away the water; it sparkled on the dry earth, and then sank in. I watched her, rocking Mandy, and my mother went back into the house.

How long was that after Colin died? Two months, maybe.

I smoke some of the joint, not much. The baby's crying, and I hear the whine of a car coming up the track in low gear and then the crunch of its tyres. I see bits of Richard's body in bright flashback, disconnected, and myself too, my hands pulling off my clothes and then flexing against the ground. I feel like someone who is running faster and faster but still finding breath.

Chapter Thirteen

Margery Wilkinson's sitting in the kitchen, holding the baby while Susan makes a pot of coffee. Her eyes rest on me, bright and curious, and I wonder what Susan's been telling her. She holds the baby expertly, even I can see that. She's wrapped his cotton shawl differently, tight, like a swaddling shawl. You'd think he'd be too hot, but he looks much more comfortable with her than he does with any of us. He's wide awake, his big navy eyes scanning her face.

'Wide awake and not crying,' I say. 'There's a miracle.'

'It's just a knack,' Margery says. 'I've had four, don't forget.'

You wouldn't guess it to look at her. Like Susan, she's blond, but in Margery's case it's an expensive blondness that has to be renewed every three weeks or so. She always wears a lot of gold jewellery; once she told Isabel she was collecting gold. Isabel's been half-promised a sight of the collection, though of course you have to be careful with insurance premiums the way they are these days. Margery is a carefully dieted woman, too, who still looks good in her jeans and white shirt.

'I haven't seen your sister,' she says to me, a faint accusation in her voice. 'She's gone to sleep, Susan says.'

'She's supposed to rest a lot.'

'Apparently she's been playing cards with someone called Edward half the morning. I don't call that resting.'

'Oh good,' I say, 'she must have been feeling better.'

'You had quite a party here last night, so Susan was telling me. I didn't realize you were such a keen cook, Nina. You'll have to give me some new ideas. I get sick of my own cooking, don't you? But of course it's different if you haven't got a family. I've the Young Farmers' barbecue next week, and my boys'll play war if it's not better than last year's. Of course Susan'll help me out, but you wouldn't believe the amount they eat. This baby's hungry, look at him.'

The baby is mouthing her shirt, making mewing sounds. 'He wants his bottle,' says Margery, staring hard at Susan.

'Mum, he's breast-fed.' Her tone makes it clear they've had all this before.

'Oh I know it's all the fashion these days. But I can tell you, Susan, when you've got three under four the way I had you'll be glad of bottles. At least you can see what they're getting. I should have taken out shares in Ostermilk.'

'He's doing fine. The health visitor weighed him and he's put on four ounces.'

'You can weigh him all you like, but he looks hungry to me and I know a hungry baby when I see one.' Her rings flash as she shifts the baby to her other arm.

'Give him your finger to suck, Mum, that'll keep him quiet.'

'What do *you* think, Nina? Doesn't it seem daft to you, your sister breast-feeding when she's had a hysterectomy? How is she going to get her strength back?'

'It's what she wants to do.'

'She doesn't know *what* she wants. How can she? You don't know if you're coming or going after a first baby. And a major operation on top of it, it's not surprising she's in the state she is.'

In the state she is. What's Susan been saying? 'And it's not just the physical side of things. You're going to have to watch out for this postnatal depression.' She watches me as I move round the kitchen. 'It's nice she's got a sister to come down. I only ever had Geoffrey's mother, and that was a very mixed blessing, I can tell you. There are some people you want near you when you're not quite yourself, and she wasn't one of them. Who is this Edward, then?'

'Oh, he's an old friend of Isabel's. You must have met him before, he's always coming down.'

'I *see*.'

I catch Susan's eye over her mother's head and Susan winks, a little fleeting wink which is much more sophisticated than anything I've ever heard her say.

'And here's Richard,' says Margery, turning, crossing her legs, 'back from foreign parts. Where was it this time?'

'Korea.'

He slides easily into a chair by Margery's.

'Do you want coffee, Richard?' I ask, unhooking more mugs.

'Yes, why not?'

'That plane must have been over us ten times yesterday if it came over once. Doesn't it drive you mad?' asked Margery, stirring sweetener into black coffee. 'I wonder it stays in the air, it's so slow.'

'I heard they were going to close down,' says Susan.

'What, Damiano's Dreamworld? Never. It's been going since you were six. We took you for your birthday the month it opened, don't you remember?'

'I wonder if anyone's done a survey,' says Richard, 'into the effectiveness of aeroplane advertising?'

'Don't suggest it,' says Margery. 'Now we've got two so-called universities down the road instead of one, half the world's surveying the other half. I'm only grateful Susan went into something sensible. The world's her oyster, isn't it, Susan?'

'Yes,' says Susan.

'I'd love to go to Damiano's Dreamworld,' I say.

'We could all go, when Isabel's better. And we'll make a point of telling them we only came because of the aeroplane.'

'It would certainly do Isabel good to get out more,' says Margery, with more meaning in her voice than I like. 'Richard, *you* ought to have a word with her. This baby's starving. Look at him, gnawing my arm with his little gums. And Susan's not thought to get so much as a tin of milk in the house, let alone a bottle.'

'Isabel doesn't want him to have any,' says Richard.

'Well, she isn't going to know, is she, if Susan gives him a little bottle when he's hungry?' Margery's eyes gleam. 'You could always tell her later on, when she's better.'

I bend down, and put my awkward hands round the baby. 'I'll take him.' I lift him carefully away from Margery, but not too carefully. I've noticed how firmly Margery grasps him, and how he seems to like it. I tuck him into the crook of my arm, and begin to walk him up and down. He doesn't cry. His eyes stare at me without quite seeming to see me, and then suddenly they droop and close fast over his eyes. 'There,' I say, 'he's asleep. He must have been tired.' I look up and see Richard watching me, his eyes moving over my body as if matching it against some pattern in his head. I look back, briefly. I'm still wearing the shorts he pulled down. I cover my thoughts so that Margery won't see them with her round, bright eyes.

'You ought to put him down now he's off,' says Susan. 'We don't want him to get used to being held all the time, do we?'

'God forbid,' says Richard. 'He'll have a terrible time when he grows up. Bring him through, Nina, and I'll open the doors for you.'

'He could go in the carrycot in my room,' says Susan; 'then you won't wake Isabel.'

'OK.' Richard holds the kitchen door open, and I pass under his arm holding the baby. Just as I do so I realize that it's his baby I'm carrying. Richard's child. I've always thought of the baby as Isabel's alone. I glance back, towards him, but I catch Margery looking at me, taking in the three of us, Richard, the baby, me. She knows nothing. She's just letting her instincts play on us and seeing what they come up with. She probably doesn't even know she's doing it. It's people like Margery you have to look out for.

Richard and I walk carefully as far as the stairs, as if Margery's still with us.

'I can manage Susan's door fine. You go back now.'

'You won't know how to turn on the baby alarm.'

He comes up behind me. Susan's room is beyond the bathroom, badly planned so that a turn of corridor cuts off about a quarter of its space. It has a single pine bed, a chest with a TV on it, a table and chair looking over the garden. Sometimes the baby sleeps in here, so that Isabel isn't disturbed. There's a carrycot on the floor, and his changing things on a trolley with a mobile of zoo animals hanging over it. All the furniture is new and quite unlike anything in the rest of the house. There's a teddy on the bed, and a pile of magazines. I lay the baby on his side, and loosen the shawl. He's gathered into himself, fast asleep, and he doesn't move as I settle him. Then I straighten up.

'There. We'd better get back.' Richard stretches out a hand, but I step back.

'Not in the house.'

'I just wanted to touch you.'

'I'm going back to the kitchen now. When Margery's gone I'll be out under the cherry tree behind the compost heap. It's nice there.'

His face looks hard, heavy and tired. He glances down at the baby and then back at me. 'Do you really want to?'

'Of course.'

Back in the kitchen Margery and Susan are pouring themselves second mugs of coffee.

'He's gone down.'

'Good,' says Susan. 'He ought to sleep till lunchtime now.'

'Your sister'll get a nice rest,' adds Margery, picking up her coffee, drinking it, looking at me. 'I must say, Nina, you're looking *very* well, I don't think I've ever seen you looking so well. Though I wouldn't have thought of you as a shorts person.'

'They're easy in this weather,' I say, 'and it doesn't matter what you wear down here, does it?' I notice that she's unable to stop herself glancing down at her crisp white shirt. Her mouth moves slightly, as if she'd like to tell me how much it costs and how tricky it is to iron. But instead she recrosses her legs and says, 'I suppose you *are* on a sort of holiday.'

The joint has made me hungry, and there are almond slices in the cake tin above Margery's head, if Edward hasn't found them. I reach up, leaning over her, and bring down the tin. It's light, too light. I open it and there is only one slice left, with the glacé cherry picked out of it.

'I was going to offer you some cake,' I say, 'but there's nothing left except this bit. Oh dear, it's gone stale. Never mind, I'll finish it off.'

The cake is delicious, synthetically moist and sweet. I eat it quickly and put the tin in the sink.

'Oh well, time for work.'

'Are you going to do some drawings, Nina?' asks Susan.

'I'd love to see them,' says Margery. 'Susan's been telling me about all this drawing. I thought you were a photographer, but now it turns out you're an artist as well.'

'I'm going to draw in the garden,' I say.

'Does being watched put you off?' asks Susan, her face turning a slightly deeper pink.

'It does rather.' I break a banana off a bunch and smile at Margery.

'Goodbye. I don't expect I'll still be here next time you come.'

'You never know,' says Margery. I'm sure it's just one of the things she says all the time, but it sounds as if she means to sit there, on and on, watching what we do, gathering evidence.

Richard is already under the tree. 'Nina –'

'It's not going to be any good if you talk,' I say.

The talking rises in his eyes, and dies down. The cherry tree is a better place than the bench, with its fermenting smell of compost, its shade and soft earth.

'But I need to pee first,' I say.

'You could go behind the tree. I shan't watch.'

'Or here.'

'Can you do that? I'd be too tense in front of you.'

He watches me, his hands stopped in undoing his belt. Suddenly he shivers. 'Jesus, Nina. You should be careful.'

'I've already told you I'm careful.'

'No, I mean, some blokes would think they could do anything.'

'But you don't think that.'

'I don't know what to think.'

'I don't know what "anything" means.'

'I could show you.'

'You could show me.'

The earth under the cherry tree is soft and warm where layers of grass cuttings have been thrown. I'm on my face, like a swimmer bruised from a slow crawl up pebbles against the drag of the sea. I roll over and look straight up at the sky, cut into chinks by wide-ribbed cherry leaves. The sky is white, the cherry leaves black. It's nearly noon, the hour when ghosts walk, and this hot summer I can see why. When I go down the track at noon I feel as if I'm dwindling, without a shadow, my head forced into my shoulders by the sun. That's how a ghost knows it's a ghost, because it makes no mark on the earth where it walks.

Richard's eyes are shut. His hands lie at his sides, unclenched, palms upward. His chest moves regularly with his breathing, but his mouth is closed and I don't think he's asleep. He looks content, fucked out. I like his silence.

I can remember Colin's funeral. His coffin was so small that my father carried it down the aisle of the small white church, as if it was a baby. My mother had told me it wouldn't really be Colin in the box, just his body, which he didn't need any more. I nodded, but I didn't know what she meant. After my bath that night, the night before the funeral, I curled up in my towel behind the bathroom door, smelling my own smell, nuzzling the warmth of my legs and arms. Isabel was sitting on the lavatory by the bath, straining to go. I watched her face flush, and then turn pale. I tried to think of me and Isabel without bodies, but I couldn't.

I don't know where the church was, but I know it wasn't in St Ives. There were a lot of people there, but no other children, and when my father walked down towards the door with the coffin there was a murmuring noise, like leaves, as people turned their heads towards him and then away. My mother was there too, at his side, her head down, wearing a dress I'd never seen before. That was important, because I knew the feel and smell of all her dresses. The green velvet with the velvet rose on the hip was my favourite, but she only wore it on special occasions. She should have been wearing it now, instead of that crinkly black stuff that smelled of shops. After we all came in I was lifted on to a seat with other people who must have been friends, but I can't remember who they were.

I was there, but Isabel wasn't; it's the only important memory from my childhood where she doesn't feature. She was in bed. For weeks after Colin's death Isabel had terrible stomach pains, so bad that sometimes she couldn't breathe. My mother would make little meals for her on a tray. Once she had two delicate lamb cutlets with a pool of mint sauce on the side. It was grown-up, expensive food, but she wasted it. I saw the tray on the kitchen table, with white lamb fat sticking the chops to the plate. I think that was the beginning of Isabel not eating with us.

Richard's fallen asleep now. He looks older, his chin sinking into the flesh under it. We talked a bit, not much. He asked how old I was, he knew I was younger than Isabel but he couldn't remember how much. I told him I was twenty-nine.

'And I'm forty-six,' he said. 'Well into the era of dental floss and bleeding from orifices.' He smiled and I saw lots of fillings in his back teeth.

A leaf detaches itself from the tree, spins down and falls on him. I wait for another. Drought's hitting the trees now, after burning grass and bushes brown. The trees survive by seeming to die: they're shedding their leaves in self-protection, drawing all their sap back to the heart. It's like an early autumn, but a strange autumn with the sun blazing on a fall of crisp brown leaves.

I get up very quietly. I've got no shadow here either, because we're already in shade, so nothing passes over his face to wake him. I pick up my clothes and shake them out, and then put them on. Already, with the fallen leaves on his chest, Richard looks as if he's been lying there a long time. It doesn't matter if anyone else finds him here lying naked on the ground, alone. People do strange things when it's as hot as this.

Chapter Fourteen

'I feel wonderful.' Isabel's up, dressed, sitting on the bed fastening her sandal. She's wearing a very pale green dress, and she's brushed her hair up on top of her head and fixed it with a comb. She looks cool and happy.

'I slept all night, and then I woke up early and played piquet with Edward and I've been asleep for another two hours at least. I feel like a different person.'

'The baby's asleep in Susan's room.'

'I thought I might take him out after lunch.' Isabel looks up at me with her long, clear look. She has the blue eyes that should belong to a blond, but set in her golden face they look strange, unsettling, as if their clarity is part of a deception.

'But you haven't got a pram.'

'I'll take him in the sling, like Susan does. Edward's going to come with me.'

'Where will you go?'

'Nowhere much. Round the garden, maybe down the track a bit.' Her eyes widen. Her face is so calm that it would be impossible to guess how frightened she is, unless you knew her. She feels better and she's going to test herself, as she must have done the other morning when she came back with her shoes soaked. I hope Edward knows what's going on.

'Are you sure you're up to it?' I ask casually, as if the only thing that worries me is the operation she's had.

'I'm supposed to walk. I was thinking back and you won't believe it, Neen, you know what I'm like about the garden, but I realized I hadn't been outside since he was born.'

Isabel is a very good actor. She mimics perfectly the surprise anyone might feel suddenly realizing she's been housebound for days.

'You've had a major operation,' I say. 'It's not surprising.'

She looks at me gratefully. 'I know. I keep forgetting. I keep thinking I ought to be doing things.'

'You mustn't push yourself.' I want Isabel to be well and happy, free to go where she wants. And I want to keep Isabel out of the garden, which is becoming my territory.

'I think I must,' she says quietly. Her hands are flat on the bed at her sides, ready to push herself up. She's still moving cautiously, afraid to wake pain.

'The baby,' I say suddenly. 'I've only just realized. I knew he reminded me of someone.'

'Who?'

'He looks like Colin.'

'Colin?' Isabel's face goes quite still, then her mouth falls open so that for a second she looks not beautiful at all. For a moment I'm terribly afraid that she's going to say, *Who is Colin?* She licks her lips. 'Colin. Do you think so?'

'It's been nagging at me ever since I first saw him. I thought he looked like Dad and of course he does, but then Colin looked like Dad as well. Everyone said so.'

'I don't remember what Colin looked like,' says Isabel.

'You must do. You were older than me, and I remember him. '

'No. I've never been able to. If I shut my eyes and try to see his face all I see is a sort of –' she pauses, shuts her eyes, 'disc.'

'I can remember him quite well.' I frown, doubting myself now. 'At least, I think I can. He was big and fair. But I suppose he might have looked big to me because I was little too. His head was wobbly.'

'Don't let's talk about it, Neen.'

'I'm sorry, Isabel, I didn't mean –'

'You forget,' she says sharply, angrily, 'I've got a baby myself now. Of course I'm going to worry about cot-death. I would anyway, let alone after what happened to Colin. Do you think I haven't thought it might happen to him? I think about it every single night when I put him down.'

'I didn't mean it like that.' A feeling stirs in me, like something coming to life, but I don't know if I can explain it to Isabel. 'It's not a sad thing. He's not going to die like Colin, I know he isn't. It's the thought that Colin hasn't really gone, not completely. You know what it was like, it seemed as if he'd just disappeared. You remember how we looked in his room and the cot was gone, and everything. And Mum never being happy again, it all seemed completely pointless.' It's only at that moment, as I say those words, that I admit to myself that my mother never was happy again after Colin's death. She worked, she looked after us, she smiled, she had friends, but her happiness had gone. I never wanted to believe it. I would sit in her lap more than I'd ever done, playing with a long necklace of amber that she had, warming the beads in my hand, singing and humming like a little girl who was happy.

'It was pointless,' says Isabel. 'I don't see why you want to talk about it.'

Her sureness stamps down on the stirring thing that I can't quite put into words. Perhaps all I remember is a disc, too. But I don't think so. I don't easily forget anything I've seen, once I've really looked at it. I remember a baby's face, turned sideways in a cot.

I'd tiptoed in alone, feeling guilty because Isabel never played with the baby and I always wanted to be the same as Isabel. But I also wanted to see him. He was awake, but not crying, peeping through the cot bars at some dancing light on the opposite wall. There was so much light when we were growing up, coming up off the sea so that even on a grey day my eyes stung with it. The baby moved his head, hearing me come in, and then a big gummy smile spread across his face. I peered in at him through the bars. His arms and legs waved like weed in a rockpool. He could turn his head but he couldn't roll over. There was a special smell all round his cot, a baby smell. He dabbed at a string of cotton reels my mother had hung across the cot, but his fist went wide. Both his legs kicked in the air and he turned to me and smiled again. His head was lying on a muslin nappy which my mother would put over her shoulder later. His hair stuck up in sweaty feathers. I stood there for quite a long time, and then I went away.

Edward opens the door without knocking. 'He's woken up, Isabel. Susan's changing him, then if you feed him we can go straight out.' He's got the sling dangling from one hand.

'All right, I'll just –' says Isabel, and she hurries out of the room.

'She looks awful,' says Edward, staring after her. 'What's happened? She was fine when she woke up.' He drops the sling on the bed, a bright coil of nursery stripes. Then he turns to me with an edge of real dislike in his voice. 'What have you been saying to her?'

'Nothing.'

'You don't think I notice anything, do you, Nina?'

'You come across as fairly self-absorbed, yes.'

'Not where Isabel's concerned.'

'Jesus, Edward, what is this thing about Isabel? Anybody would think you were in love with her. If they didn't know you.'

'I do love Isabel, as it happens. Isn't it interesting, Nina – you think you're so liberated, but really all you see when you look at me is "Isabel's gay friend". You can't look beyond that.'

'It's not that I can't. It's that I'm not interested enough to do so.'

'You're not all that interested in Isabel, either, are you? I think you're a shit, Nina, but since she doesn't see through you I'll keep my thoughts to myself.'

I'm bad at dealing with people who don't like me. A bit of me wants them to, even though I know it's not going to happen, and I don't like them at all myself. And I've always found it

84

unbearable to think of affection flowing towards Isabel, and a blank face turned to me. But I fight it now. I can be hard and cold.

'You do that,' I say. 'Isabel and I are sisters. We share a past that you don't know anything about and can't possibly understand.'

'I hope that's all you share,' says Edward.

The words gleam, so double-edged they cut wherever they touch.

I watch them from Isabel's window, walking down the paths. The sling is round Edward, because the pull of it was uncomfortable for her. They look small and happy, walking slowly to and fro across the lawn, bending to look at things which are too small for me to see, disappearing down paths, between shrubs, and then reappearing. Once, I hear Isabel laugh. Beyond the wall the meadows are bleached, with a diagonal green scar running across one of them where there must be water just under the ground. I move to the side of the window, where I can see and not be seen, and just then Isabel and Edward come out of the trees and walk towards the house. Edward stops and hitches at the sling, trying to adjust it, but it fastens at the back. Isabel goes behind him and fiddles with the clip while he bends at the knees to make it easier for her. When she's made the adjustment they both turn to look down the garden, with their backs to me, shading their eyes against the glare of the midday sun. On the back of Isabel's pale-green dress, between her shoulder-blades, there is a dark patch of sweat.

Chapter Fifteen

The sea was there all the time. I would wake in the night and listen to the sea until it took me back into sleep. When we were older Isabel and I slept in the attic that ran the length of our narrow terraced house, our beds under each of the dormer windows. We looked out over Porthmeor Beach, over the Island, at the shining trail left on the sea by fishing boats heading west from the harbour. On winter nights storms punched the wall by my ear and our house shuddered before the wind. If the storm came by day Isabel and I would go out in it, in our yellow oilskins and hats, to watch the sea boil and the spray explode at the base of the cliffs.

The sea got into everything. Our leather school sandals were white with salt before we'd had them a week. Later they would rot at the seams, long before we'd grown out of them. There was sand in the carpets, sand in the grass. Every year my mother would slap paint on every window-frame she could reach, so that the sea would not eat down to the wood. Wind and salt scoured off paint and covered the windows with spray. Our hair was sticky, whipped into tangles until we couldn't get a comb through it. Each summer one streak bleached white over my forehead. In winter there were thick white mists that clung to us like cobwebs, and the noise of a foghorn lowing; then the air would begin to move again and black humps of rock would slide out of the silence. When the fog was heavy I kept my mouth shut, frightened that it would get into my throat and choke me. But Isabel danced ahead, just out of sight, daring the fog to swallow her up. Our father had a rhyme for Isabel:

Isabel, Isabel, met a bear;
Isabel, Isabel, didn't care . . .

I thought he'd made it up for her, and was surprised to find it in a book years later, with someone else's name under it.

He was often away. He was a poet, but not the poet he wanted to be. He was a very good critic, and he couldn't stop being one when he looked at his own work. I still try to read his poems sometimes. You can find his collections in second-hand bookshops, and they don't cost very much. There's something terrible about the way titles of books fade. He wrote poems about us, but he didn't see us very much. He had to spend a lot of time in London, where he did his reviewing and critical articles. St Ives was my mother's place, and if he wasn't there too much I suppose he could avoid seeing how much better she was as a potter than he was as a poet. Although I don't think he was the sort of man who could easily avoid seeing things.

He was a handsome man, our father, and five years younger than my mother. He was fair, with the same eyes as Isabel, the same golden skin, which was creased by the time I knew him. By some reckonings my mother was lucky to get him. He drew people round him, because he was funny, because he had the way of making you feel that you were something new and delightful he'd just discovered, and above all because there was something lost and pained in him which people felt without knowing quite what it was. He seemed to need you. My mother didn't seem to need anybody much. Only after Colin died I heard her cry out, behind a door, and I thought she'd called my name. I slid the door open. It was dark because the curtains were pulled over the window, but I could see her. She was lying on her face, clutching the pillow. Her head thumped from side to side. My father was sitting on the bed, smoking a cigarette, and he saw me because the light changed as I opened the door. My mother didn't notice. He just looked up and shook his head slightly, and I went out again.

A bit later she went away for a while. My father looked after us on his own, the only time I can remember him doing that. We loved every minute of it. A weight had gone out of the house, and though Isabel still had stomach pains and didn't eat much, she seemed much happier once our mother had gone. He didn't cook at all. In the mornings we had cornflakes, at lunch-time we had money for fish and chips, at night he took us out. Things must have been going quite well then. There seemed to be money for going out and for real shopping. Sometimes we just had what we couldn't do without, fetched each day from the corner shop by me and Isabel.

We went out late, because my father hated eating early. We had steak and chips, or spaghetti. Isabel ate, too. I watched her out of the corner of my eye when the waitress put the plate of steaming sauce and wriggly spaghetti down in front of her, the first night. But she ate it, wrapping up the pasta on her fork expertly, in a way I couldn't manage. I forgot to eat my own food, stopped in my tracks by Isabel's cleverness.

The next night the waitress leaned over me and whispered to us, 'I've got something you'll like.' She brought two plates from behind her back. On each there was a chocolate teddy-bear, gleaming brown. Their skin had a mist of cold on it.

'It's ice-cream inside,' said the waitress and watched us, smiling. I picked up my spoon but it was too beautiful to eat.

'Go on. It'll only melt.'

I tapped the chocolate as if it was a boiled egg. Immediately tiny cracks sprayed over the chocolate, showing the white ice-cream underneath. I looked at Isabel to see what she was doing, but she hadn't touched hers. Isabel was always able to wait for things. This was different though. Her hands had dropped to her lap and her face was closed. She wasn't going to eat it.

'Don't you like it?' the waitress asked Isabel. Her voice was cross with disappointment.

'I'd rather have fruit salad,' said Isabel in a tiny thread of a voice. Saying nothing, the waitress swept up the plate with the chocolate teddy-bear on it, and bounced out. I dug deep into mine and began to eat fast, hardly tasting it, hoping I'd have finished it by the time the waitress got back.

Isabel's salad looked sour. Our father gave the waitress one of his big, soft smiles. 'You're very good,' he said, 'but I don't think she feels much like eating at the moment. She's still upset.'

The waitress's face went weak, and she nodded, looking at Isabel in a quite different way. 'Of course, the little one's too young to feel it the same,' she said. I ate on, my face burning, the chocolate teddy-bear slipping round the plate as I chased it with my spoon.

Once the waitress had gone our father hummed to himself, quietly,

Isabel, Isabel, met a bear;
Isabel, Isabel didn't care . . .

I loved his face when it crinkled up with laughing, or with trying not to laugh. He seemed to find us funny most of the time, even when we weren't trying to be. Soon after this he told me he was thinking of starting a pudding club, and I could be in it if I liked. The only rule was that members had to discover at least four new puddings a year. I didn't see how I was going to discover any puddings, as I had no money of my own, but he told me that one day he would take me to London and we'd go to a place where they did nothing else but puddings. When I was big and had learned to read he would buy me a book of puddings and I could learn to cook them.

'It's no good relying on your mother and Isabel. They're fruit salads, the pair of them.'

Of course my father had a woman in London, and she wasn't

a fruit salad. I met her later on; she was called Amy Ludgate. He married her for a year after my mother's death, before he died too. My mother had expected to die, because she'd had breast cancer for two years, but my father hadn't. He went out almost between one step and the next, on his way back from the launch of someone else's new collection. It was an aneurysm, a weakness no one had known about. He hadn't made a will and there wasn't any money, but Amy offered us his manuscripts. She was sure they'd be worth a lot of money one day. Besides, we were his daughters and she thought we had a right to them, whatever the law said. She was generous, Amy. She could love things and not want to own them. She never stopped fighting the battles against neglect that my father would not fight for himself. But we knew no one was ever going to care for his poetry as much as she did, so we said she should keep the manuscripts, and she has them still. I had a letter from her not long ago saying she'd made her will, and naming the university library she had chosen to have his papers. I only hope they're willing to take them.

He'd been with Amy before Colin was born. Colin was a fluke, not an attempt at reconciliation. I found out later that my parents hadn't slept together for two years before he was born. But my father was down from London for a few days and they sat for a long time over a meal after we went to bed, drinking rich red wine that my father had brought back from France. And so they stumbled into bed and later there was Colin. No, not stumbled. They weren't that drunk, my mother said. They still knew what they were doing. It was very important to her to be accurate about things like that, and not to give us false ideas about what had happened between them. I suppose it was a good thing, but it could feel a bit bleak. Colin was born, and then he died, and his death brought them closer than his life had done, for a while.

My father wrote a poem which was read at Colin's funeral. I didn't understand a word of it and I couldn't work out why he was suddenly standing up at the front and reading it, when I knew this wasn't a poetry reading. One odd thing followed another, like strange fish you have to separate from the catch and throw back.

I can still taste that chocolate teddy-bear. Cold, sweet, tender, the splintered chocolate giving way to smoothness. In fact I can taste it better now than I could then as I rushed to please the waitress. I see us all: Isabel poking at a segment of tinned grapefruit with her face in shadow as her long hair slipped forwards; my father smoking and chatting to the waitress over our heads; and me kicking the chair legs and waiting for someone to admire my nice clean plate.

When both your parents are dead great slabs of the past drop away like eroded cliffs. I want my past back. I need it now, to ask it the questions I never realized I needed to ask. But there's nothing. Silence, and the shining of the sea where once there was land. I have Isabel's stories. She's made a story of the past which I used to accept without question. She's so persuasive that it doesn't seem like persuasion, but like the truth. Edward is persuaded. There they are, walking again side by side, but even more slowly now, as if the heat of the sun is pressing them down. No. It's not that. Something's wrong. She isn't walking right. I lean forward and push up the window and at the same moment Edward grabs Isabel's arm, but she buckles away from him, very slowly, her body folding up and dropping to the grass. He kneels. The baby's in the way, the sling hampers him. He can't get at her, can't lift her and turn her over. He turns, looking for help, and sees me watching.

Chapter Sixteen

Isabel should never have gone outside. The sun at midday is hotter than it's been for two hundred years. Ladybirds swarm, clay-puddled dew ponds crack in the heat, empty. The Downs are yellow-brown, like the flanks of lions. At midday the emptiness of the sky and the pounding of the sun are frightening. But then evening comes, and the light liquefies to yellow and Isabel's absent, knocked out.

It's evening now. Past nine, getting dark, and I'm in the garden. I'm watering Isabel's apple trees bucket by bucket, because it's forbidden to use a hose. I'm thinking of Isabel and sickness. The afternoon's been full of it, the doctor coming, the midwife calling in to check up, the health visitor advising Isabel on feeding. Isabel says she wants to stop breast-feeding the baby now. It's making her ill. The health visitor says she's doing so well, she mustn't give up. 'Mustn't?' says Isabel, and she shuts her eyes, turning her silky brown shoulder on everyone. Later she tells Richard to drive into town and buy bottles and tinned milk. Everything turns on Isabel. And hasn't it always done, since she lay in bed, in pain, while our brother was buried.

I am sick of it all. Milk and blood and babies. I lug another bucket down the path, the dark water shivering inside it. Water slops over my bare feet and raises scent from the dust. These trees should never have been planted in a drought. I heft the bucket and walk on, all my skin prickling with attention. I'm waiting. I leave the full bucket standing by the trees and wander on through the gloom, down to the raspberry canes. There are big moths flying. When they land patches of white show up on their wings so they look like jigsaws. Daytime life closes down, and night life begins with its own excitement. I wish I was in the city now, where day and night brush each other for hours. I wish I was in a taxi, hurtling round the corners of parks as they turn from blue to black with dusk.

There's a tall, thick double row of canes. Some have finished fruiting, others are still in season. I feel for berries in the dark and find them, their ripe seeds melting on my tongue. I hear feet on the path behind me but I keep on picking, prolonging that moment of not looking round.

It's gone much darker. Most of the garden has been gulped down into shadow, but white flowers glow across it.

'Give me one,' Richard asks.

I pick off a berry and hold it to his lips. He's half-opened his mouth, ready.

'I could have given you anything,' I say. 'What if that was deadly nightshade?'

'You wouldn't do that.'

'What's going on?'

'Nothing. Isabel's asleep. They've moved the baby into the cot because the health visitor thought he'd sleep better.'

I move away, down the row.

'Come here.'

'I'm picking raspberries for tomorrow.'

'What are you wearing? I can't see.'

'My blue dress. The short one.'

'I'll help you.'

He pushes after me down the hollow grassy passage between the raspberry canes. I want to run but I make myself keep still, feeling under the leaves for the slight furriness of the fruit. The berries are warmer than the leaves. He touches my arm but I twist and move on.

'Nina.'

'Yes.'

He's behind me, his hands running up my thighs under my dress. I lean back against him, opening my legs, aching.

'Do you want another?'

He opens his mouth and I push in raspberries. His hand is between my thighs, feeling for the opening of my vagina. He slides in a finger, two fingers. I turn my cheek against his arm. He's changed from a white to a denim shirt and I know why. The glint of a white shirt carries a long way through the dusk.

'You want it.'

'You know I do.'

'That's what you came here for.'

'Of course it is.'

He sighs, and we slide down. It's damp here, between the canes, and dark. He's kicking off his jeans, and I pull up my dress.

'Not like that. Take all your clothes off like you did last time.'

It's a loose, short dress and it comes off easily. I roll it into a ball and toss it out of the way.

'That's better.'

We lie lengthways between the canes, hot, slippery, naked.

'Say what you said before.'

'What?'

'Say we can always have a good fuck.'

'I don't need to. You know it already.'

'But say it.'

'We can always fuck.'

'Always.'

'When we want.'

'Now.'

He lies underneath me. I ease myself down on to him slowly and we start to move. I'm on an endless staircase, going down, going nowhere.

I fall asleep for a minute afterwards, a brief skim through sleep that's snatched away as soon as it begins. Richard's moving, rolling me away. He gets up and crawls down the canes into the open.

'What're you doing?'

'Looking for your dress.'

I brush the earth off me and go out after him. He's sweeping the ground with his hands, but every patch of shadow looks like something that's fallen.

'What if you don't find it?'

'I'll find it.'

He scoops, pouncing. 'Here it is.'

There's enough light for us to see each other's pale nakedness. He lifts the dress and shakes it out. Then he crouches down with the dress between his hands.

'What are you doing? Richard, what're you doing with my dress?'

I hear him strain and grunt and the soft cotton rips.

'You've torn my dress.'

He laughs, turns the dress round, rips it again.

'You bastard.'

'You don't mind. You don't really mind.'

'What did you do that for?'

He kicks the dress away, stands up. 'So you can't go back in the house.'

'I'll tear up your bloody jeans then.'

'You can't. They're too strong.'

'You'll find out.'

We grapple, swaying. Suddenly I slip my hands down and squeeze his balls, hard.

'Christ, Nina! That hurts.'

'You don't mind,' I say; 'you like me hurting you.'

'I like everything you do,' he says.

'Isn't that nice.'

'Wait a minute.' He tenses, his body concentrating inwards the way men do while they check if they're getting an erection or not.

'No, not now you've ripped up my dress.'

'I'll get you another one.'

'You won't. I buy my own clothes.'

'I want you to be naked.'

'It's dark. You can't see me.'

'That doesn't matter.'

I don't often get to the point where I forget who I am. Where I end, where the other person begins. You have to go on for a long time and it's not a matter of emotions, it's a physical thing. I got there with Richard.

'We can't go inside like this,' I said later, 'we smell of fucking.'

'You could put on my shirt.'

'That'd be worse than nothing, wouldn't it? I know. Come on.'

I pull him with me towards Isabel's new apple trees. I feel the zinc bucket with my foot, see the faint shine of water.

'Stand still. Now, whatever I do, don't make a sound. Shut your eyes.'

I can't see if he shuts them or not. I bend, taking the weight of the heavy bucket with my thigh muscles. The water heaves up one side.

'Bend down.'

I stand very close to him, hoist up the bucket as high as I can and up-end it over us both, as slowly as I can so that water runs in a cold, steady stream over thighs and shoulders and breasts.

'Wash me with it,' I say, and keep on pouring while he lathers the water over me.

'Wait a minute. Open your legs.'

'I've had enough, Richard.'

'I'm only going to wash you.' He scoops a handful of water, washes my vulva as gently and quickly as a nurse. 'Now you do me.' I pass him the half-full bucket and then I wash his penis, his balls, the sweat and semen trapped in his hair.

'There, you're clean.'

Richard dresses slowly, while I watch.

'Come on, put this round you. You'll get cold.'

I put on his shirt, and button it. It's long enough to cover my thighs and if I meet anyone, why should they guess it doesn't belong to me?

'What time is it?'

'Eleven.'

'Only eleven?'

'Yes. Nina –'

I can hear it in his voice, the talk that's got to come.

'I'm tired, Richard, I want to get to bed.'

'I know. But there's things we've got to sort out. I'm away tomorrow.'

'I told you I don't want to talk.'

'Nina,' he says, holding my wrists, 'it's not going to work like that. Fucking in the garden and nothing in the house. You're kidding yourself. I know what your cervix feels like, for Christ's sake. I've watched you pissing. I'm buggered if we're not going to talk.'

Cervix, I think briefly, impressed. As an index of intimacy not many men would think of that. There was that TV programme where blindfold men had to pin the clitoris on to a drawing of a woman's fanny. Like pinning the tail on a donkey, only they weren't as accurate. One got it right, more or less right, and came out tapping the side of his nose. *Married man*, he said. I love things like that. Then I remember that of course Richard knows about cervices. There was Isabel's, opening up to give birth.

'Then I'm going back to London,' I say.

He lets go of my wrists abruptly so my hands slap against my thighs and walks away a few feet. I wait. At last he says, in a dry, different voice, 'You certainly are sisters, aren't you?'

'What do you mean?'

'You give with one hand and you take back with the other.'

I pull his shirt round me. 'I'm going in.'

'Go on then.'

Edward's waiting for me as I come through the kitchen door in the dark.

'I thought you'd come this way,' he says. All my blood runs back to my heart, then shocks up to my skin. Edward turns on the light and the room leaps out at me, too bright, too shiny, every surface as inquisitive as Margery Wilkinson's eyes. I look down and see dark stains on the shirt I'm wearing, like blood. Raspberry juice. My legs are scratched too, and there's dirt on them.

'I knew already,' says Edward. 'I saw you this morning. Who do you think you are? You're not in the Garden of fucking Eden, you know. I wish you could have seen yourself.'

'Sex isn't meant to be pretty for onlookers,' I say. 'You should know that. Or maybe you don't, or Alex would've stayed more than an hour.'

'I can't believe you're Isabel's sister.'

'No, you're right. I'm not at all like Isabel. I'm bad and she's good, so bear it in mind.'

I tell myself it doesn't touch me, none of this touches me. It's a game of bad tennis. But my back's against the door and I'm out of breath.

'How can you do this to her?' he asks, and this time there's no malice in it. He simply wants to know. 'She's just had a baby. She's been terribly ill. You know how vulnerable she is, or if you don't you should do. Do you really not care about Isabel at all?'

'You don't have the right to ask me that.'

And I know I've won. He looks away, flushing under his fine skin.

'There's something missing in you,' he says. I look at him but I can't make myself angry with him, can't make myself feel any of the emotions he expects and half-wants. He does love Isabel.

'So what are you going to do?' I ask and, as I expect, he doesn't answer.

I move towards the door. I can go to Isabel now, asleep or not, before anyone else does. After all, I'm her sister.

Chapter Seventeen

The lamp is on, and Isabel is standing by the cot, sideways to me as I open the door. The drop bars are down. First I notice the big roses on her silk kimono, and then her head, bent, her whole body leaning down over the child. Her hand is on him, pressing him. It seems as if all her weight is going down on him.

I open my dry mouth and my voice rasps in my throat. I see her, tall Isabel, her dark silky hair falling like bunches of grapes, her kimono brushing the floor. But I see another Isabel as well, half her height, in a cotton nightdress which comes down to her knees. This Isabel is braced, on tiptoe, leaning over the cot. Her hair is pushed back behind her ears and I can see her thin, intent face. She is pressing down on the baby's back, pressing and pressing, pushing him into the mattress. I can see his weak purple legs thrashing but there's no sound. His face is hidden in a muslin nappy. She hears me come in, she turns, she does not stop pushing the baby down. Her face is cold and hard, like a snake's face, but her voice is a soft whisper.

'He was crying. I'm getting him to sleep. Go back to our room.'

And I go. I creep back on bare feet that are suddenly cold, across the lino to the big bed I share with Isabel. I climb in and wrap the sheets tightly round me and I lie in the dark I've made, shivering until I fall asleep. When I wake up it's sunshine and morning and Isabel is on the floor, cross-legged, reading a book. She looks up and smiles at me.

The image switches off. Tall Isabel, my sister with her baby, stands by the cot patting her baby's back gently and rhythmically.

'He's got wind,' she whispers. 'He's had awful colic this evening.'

'Isabel.' I can't think of anything else to say.

'What's the matter?'

'Colin. What happened? What happened to Colin?'

But Isabel's golden face is smooth, glinting with peace. Cautiously, so as not to wake the baby, she stands back. I see Antony's perfect, sleeping face.

'What's wrong with you, Nina? You know he died of cotdeath. I can't believe how you keep going on about it when I've just had Antony. I told Edward about it and he wanted to have a word with you but I told him not to.'

She smiles. 'Isn't it wonderful when they're asleep?'

Waves of peaceful conspiracy wash over me, but this time I'm going to struggle. 'Isabel, when I saw you there –' No, that isn't the way. 'Isabel, the night Colin died. You must think back, it's important.'

'I remember it,' says Isabel. Her clear blue eyes look back at me, and there's a delicate frown cut into her forehead.

'Were you in his room? Before I woke up?'

'Was I in his room? What do you mean?'

'I mean, did you go into Colin's room? Did you stand by his cot, just like that, like you were standing by Antony's?'

'Why do you think that?' asks Isabel quickly.

'I saw it just now. You were standing there in your nightdress, the rosy nightdress. You remember, yours was pink and mine was blue. You turned round and spoke to me. You told me you were just getting the baby to sleep. "Go back to our room," that's what you said.'

'What do you mean, you saw it?'

'I saw it. I remembered it. You know how I remember things in pictures.'

She is silent, gazing back at me out of her untroubled face. But I know Isabel too well not to see the thoughts that race, flicker, dive and surface again. She takes a step towards me, and then another. Suddenly the rose silk of the kimono is round me, folding me in. Isabel is breathing hard, her breath working up into sobs. I pull away and see that there are tears on her face and more welling at the corners of her eyes.

'Oh Nina. Oh Neen,' she stammers, her fine hands clasping mine. 'I thought you'd really forgotten. I thought you wouldn't ever remember.'

'But I do remember.'

'Don't, Neen. Don't, don't. Don't remember. You were only four. It wasn't your fault. You didn't know what you were doing.'

Her big eyes swim at me, her face yearning with pity for me. I step back.

'What? What do you mean, Isabel? Of course it wasn't my fault. How could it have been my fault?'

'Do you remember everything?' she demands. She has the face of a compassionate judge.

'Of course I do.' But uncertainty runs round me like ice, taking me into a new climate. Through the fog and cold I'm beginning to see the bulk of Isabel's truth, advancing like an iceberg to blot out my world.

'You were only four,' she explains. 'You were jealous, of course you were. It was natural. That's why I never made a fuss of Colin, or held him – you must remember that, Neen. Everyone thought it was strange, because I'd loved holding you when you were a baby. But I knew you hated it when I touched him. That's why Mum didn't go on breast-feeding him, because you were so jealous. She thought it'd make you feel better if he had bottles.'

'You didn't want to hold him,' I say.

'Of course I did. I always loved babies. Then that night, do you remember? – you got into trouble because you were jumping on the bed and making a noise and you woke him up. Mum was furious. I tried to make you feel better but I didn't realize how upset you were really. Then we must have fallen asleep.'

'But you were in the bedroom,' I say. 'You were leaning over his cot.'

'Of course I was, but that was afterwards.'

'After what?'

'After I came in and found Colin. I'd heard you come back in the room and I thought you'd been to the toilet, but then I woke up properly and I knew you couldn't have, because you were frightened of the cistern so you always woke me up to take you. So I thought something must be wrong. You were very cold so I wrapped you up in bed again. But you'd left the door open. I went to shut it and I saw Colin's door was open as well. I went in and I found what you'd done. The pillow was still over his head.' I stare at Isabel, unable to speak. 'I knew they'd know it was you. Everyone'd said how jealous you were. I took off the pillow and turned him over and I knew he was dead because of the colour he'd gone. I arranged all the blankets again and put him so he looked as if he was asleep, facing the door. But when I turned round you were there. You hadn't gone back to sleep. I didn't want to frighten you so I told you Colin had woken up and I was settling him. I didn't want you to know what you'd done. I thought you'd never know. You might have forgotten it all in the morning.'

I lick my lips. 'I didn't remember,' I say in a crack of a voice.

'I knew you didn't. I could tell that in the morning. So after we'd played I pretended to go and see how Colin was. I wanted you not to think it had anything to do with you.'

'Isabel.' Fear, horror, admiration, disbelief fight in me. The iceberg slices the side of my ship, and I go down. But though I'm finished, Isabel doesn't seem to know it, and her voice patters on. 'That's why I was ill. I had to keep it all in and not tell anyone. I couldn't go to the funeral.'

'You've never, then . . . You've never – told anyone?'

'No,' she says, holding my eyes, 'of course not. I've never blamed you, Neen. I'll never blame you for anything. I love you.'

Chapter Eighteen

Nobody knows. Not Richard, not Edward. She hasn't told anyone because it was too dangerous. I was her Neen, her baby. She thought they'd take me away if they knew.

She loved me so much, I always knew that. I always knew that Isabel loved me even more than our mother did, because she told me so. Often she walked me right to the end of Smeaton's pier, when the tide was high and the fishing-boats were coming into harbour. We could look down through twenty feet of water that were as clear as jelly. If we fell we'd hang there like fruit in jelly. The wind blew, our hair flapped and she held my hand tight. The fall we might have fallen made my knees ache, but I was safe with Isabel. My mother would let her take me anywhere.

'I've had to hide it all for so long. I'm sorry, Neen. I'm so, so sorry. If you hadn't said anything I'd never have told you. But I swear I'll never tell anyone else.'

'Not even Richard?'

'No.'

And the evidence. She didn't need to tell me what would have happened to the evidence. All dissolved now, vanished underground. Colin's been buried so long. No one found any evidence then, and they never would now.

'Did the police come?' I ask. Isabel shakes her head so her hair gleams and ripples in the lamplight. Why am I thinking of how beautiful she is, now, when it's the last thing that counts?

'The doctor came.'

'Did he ask us what happened?'

'Of course not. We weren't the ones who'd found Colin. We'd been asleep all night, just like we usually were.'

'And you didn't – you never said anything to them?'

A tiny, sideways movement of Isabel's head. She watches me intently.

'Are you all right, Neen? You look awful.'

'I'm – I don't know. I don't feel like me any more.'

'It's because it was a shock. You didn't realize before. You never knew anything. I always knew you didn't.' She smiles fluently at me, offering me back my innocence. 'You could never have pretended so well. You know how they say children bury memories deep down, if something terrible happens.'

'I must have known. You can't do something like that and not know it.' I circle round the words that I can't bring myself to say. A four-year-old girl, me, put a pillow over the head of a baby and pressed down until he was dead, and then she went back into her room and slept until morning. And never said anything about it, or did anything, or remembered anything. Why don't my hands remember? Why don't my fingers ache? He must have struggled.

'You remember the games we used to play with our dolls?' says Isabel. 'They were always being ill and dying and having funerals and then coming back to life. You must have thought that would happen to Colin. You only did to him what you'd done to your doll lots of times. You didn't really know what death was.'

But I did. I went to the funeral and saw him come out in that little white box in our father's arms. The lid was down, fastened down, and it would never be taken off. I understood that and I was afraid when I looked at my mother's terrible face. I knew something about death.

'Isabel.' My voice scrapes. 'Thank you.'

Isabel's eyes widen. 'Thank you? What for?'

'Not saying anything.'

'I'll never say anything. You can trust me, Neen.'

I stare at her. The thought ripples in me that even if she did say something now, no one would believe her. There is no evidence, so it's Isabel's word against mine. Even my mother is firmly dead, and I think that only she could ever dare to put together the threads of such a story.

'Go to bed,' says Isabel. 'Go to sleep, Neen. You look worn out.'

My sister stares deep into my eyes. Her body is a column of calm and there is still a tiny half-smile on her face. All I've been thinking about since I got here is her weakness, her fragility, but now that is stripped away and it's easy to see how strong she really is. She's said nothing for twenty-five years. And not only that, she's never changed towards me. I try to think what it must be like to take the hand of a four-year-old who's killed her baby brother, and lead her back to bed. Without frightening me. And then taking away the pillow, and rearranging Colin to lie 'as if he was asleep'.

I wonder what would have happened if Isabel hadn't thought so quickly? I would have had a different life, not my own life. What life I possess, I possess because Isabel's given it to me. Isabel is my mother.

'I'll see you in the morning,' says Isabel. 'Go to sleep. We won't ever talk about it again. It'll be the same as it's always been.'

There's a tiny sigh, a huff of breath from Antony's cot.

I sleep. I am by the sea, the wind blowing, the rage of gulls in my ears. We're climbing cliffs, too high. The noise of the gulls changes into angry voices above my head. I am small and half-hidden in my mother's skirt, standing in the cold blowing street while the adults talk over me.

'I've said to myself many a time seeing your girl pass, she's too young to be let out with that pram. If Jos Quick hadn't made a grab for it your littl'un ud have been a goner.'

My mother, cold, clipped. 'It was an accident. She's very sorry.'

'I daresay. She was poking about there in the floats and nets, did you know that? Had her back to the pram though she'd gone and left it right on the edge of the pier with the brake off. Did she tell you that?'

'Of course she did.'

'She wants her backside tanned if you ask me. How old is she? Seven? Old enough to know better.'

'It won't happen again.'

The voices change. They are gulls now, not women. One of them hurtles down the air towards me, braking just above my head. I feel its claws in my hair, tangling, dragging, lifting to carry me away with it to its carrion nest on the cliffs. I wake with an icy jolt to my watch showing 4.17. The dream is so clear that I put my hand to my hair. But the voices are fading already, becoming noise, not words. A few seconds after I come out of the dream it has dissolved.

But I'm not out of sleep yet. The dream has given way to another dream. My mother stays. She isn't angry any more, but I can see her sitting on my bed, crossing her legs with a faint rasp of nylon. She must be going out somewhere, because for work she wears trousers and an overall and she smells of clay dust, not gardenia. It's evening and I'm ready for bed, but Isabel hasn't come upstairs yet. My legs are long now and my feet make a bump well down the bedclothes. I'm seven or eight. My mother looks at me and says, 'I've always known I can leave my purse anywhere in the house and you and Isabel won't touch it.' And I nod, proud, enthralled with the idea of my own honesty. 'Never mind, Nina,' she says.

'Never mind what?'

'It was just –' she looks carefully away, 'just I thought I had more money than I found I had, when I came to pay the milkman.'

'You must have spent it already.'

'Yes, I must.' She reaches over to the funny lock of hair which always flops over my face unless I stab it firmly with a kirbigrip. She strokes the hair back.

'Is my hair nearly as long as Isabel's?' I ask.

'Not quite.' My mother is always truthful. Sometimes I think less truth would make our life more comfortable.

'Is anything worrying you, Nina?' asks my mother, suddenly, surprising me. This is not her sort of question.

'No. Of course not.' I make my eyes as honest as I can in the semi-dark.

'I just thought that sometimes – it might be difficult for you, having Isabel – having an elder sister ahead of you all the time.'

'You mean, because Isabel's so good at everything.'

'Not only that.'

I try to think what my mother can possibly mean. Of course Isabel is better than me at school, but I'm used to that. Teachers remember Isabel all the way up the school and when I arrive in the class they're ready for me. I'm haunted by the ghost of her perfect copying, and by the neat way her socks stay up. I have been shown pages of Isabel's exercise books with her sums done so beautifully that the teacher has given her not only ten red stars but a silver rabbit to stick on to the book.

'Because she's got longer hair and everything?'

'Mm. No. I just wondered if you wanted to do more things on your own. Without Isabel.'

'I like being with Isabel.'

'I know you do. But you like drawing and Isabel doesn't.'

'I always do drawing while Isabel's busy.'

'Yes. But you're quite good at drawing. It won't develop unless you work on it.'

My mother sounds as if she's talking to a grown-up, not me. I wriggle round in the bed. 'You could give us lessons,' I suggest. I know that my mother doesn't mean Isabel and me, she means just me, but perversely I don't want to acknowledge that. Isabel can draw a vase of daisies and a cat watching a goldfish. And that's that. People at school hang over her desk when she does them.

'Isabel's going to tea with Katie Trevose tomorrow. Why don't you come then?' She shifts her weight. I know she'll only ask me once, because that's how my mother is. She never tries to persuade us.

'All right.'

'Good.' She pats my legs. I slide down in the bed, silent. Isabel will be coming to bed in a minute. Will she be able to smell my treachery in the air?

I am awake now. Really awake. I have got to think what to do. It's later than I thought; I must have fallen asleep again. It's ten to six and the room is light. I'm hungry.

No one else is up yet, not even the baby. There's nothing in the cupboards. Instant coffee, two packets of Weetabix, cheap jelly marmalade. Isabel grows her own vegetables, but she also has a freezer full of Mother's Pride and beef sausages. I reach into the hollow china duck where keys are kept. Yes, Richard's left his car keys.

It's nice to be back in a car, in its city smell of used-up air. I click on the radio, turn on the ignition and reverse carefully round the pond. As I come out on to the track I have the feeling I'm being watched. I keep on, driving faster than I should on the rough surface, not looking back.

Town's empty too. I park the car and walk down Wash Street towards the corner where I remember a bakery. I can smell it already, the warmth of new bread curling out into the grey streets. The grey is thinning to blue and it'll be hot again, of course. It takes so little time to get used to a climate where the sun always shines.

It's a good bakery. I buy cheese bread and a wheel of fresh

pizza in a white cardboard box, two French sticks and a sticky dark loaf with sunflower seeds in it. I buy a box of home-made shortbread, and five cream doughnuts. Susan, Richard, Edward, Nina. And Isabel. The assistant finds carrier bags and packs the stuff in. I add a pot of ginger chutney, and just then the first batch of croissants comes in on a stained metal tray and I buy twelve. I walk out, my arms, full, peering over bags and boxes. A man walking his dog smiles at me. 'You've a family to feed all right,' he says, and I nod and smile and imagine the person who might go home to the scrubbed wooden table and the Aga and the scrubbed blond children, and dump the parcels on the table saying breathlessly, 'Now, darlings, don't all grab at once . . .'

I stow the bags and get into the car. The streets are clean and empty, and I drive on a rush of exhilaration, out of the town, accelerating on to the wide white road that curves past the bottom of the Downs. The sun is up and there are fresh blue shadows at the side of the road. Over the Downs the sky is shining and the car smells of bread and pizza. The radio's playing 'Turn your back on me' . . . and then a lorry grows huge in the driving mirror, all metal teeth so close up I think it's going to hit until at the last moment it swings out. Its huge wheels thud the road alongside me, jouncing the car, taking up the whole road as a blind corner comes up fast. Its brakes hiss enormously but it keeps going, trundling beside me in a blind thunder of weight and speed. The moment stretches, the huge wheels churn in the window space beside me, so close I could put out my hand. But nothing happens. No car coming the other way, no moment where being alive explodes into what? Nothing happens. I hold the wheel tight. The windows are wide open and I hear a bird sing in the hedge on my left. Then the lorry rocks in ahead of me, straightens, drives on. I am less than half a mile from the turn-off to the track.

I turn off, and stop the car. The birds sing louder. I feel no different this morning from any other morning. It hasn't sunk in, I tell myself. I am still living as if I don't know the truth of what I am. The morning world is as new and shiny as it's ever been. The track ahead of me bulges with cows' backsides as they walk slowly, willingly, and I put the car into gear and drive behind, at their pace.

Richard's in the kitchen, giving the baby his bottle. I carry in all my bags and boxes, and kick the door shut. He looks at me, but says nothing. The baby is crumpled and tiny against his blue shirt. Richard looks up at me but his face is hard to read.

'Breakfast,' I say, dumping everything on the table.

'Smells good.'

'It'll be good. The only thing I couldn't get was coffee.'

'There's a jar in the cupboard.'

'I'm sure there is. I'm talking about coffee.'

'You're a snob, did you know that? A food snob.'

Our conversation is as tinny as an advert. I go over and stand close to him, and the baby looks up, but not at us. It occurs to me suddenly that you could do anything you liked in front of a baby. It frightens me to think of the power that comes with the birth of a child.

'He's drinking it.'

'Of course he is,' says Richard. 'He's already had two bottles in the night. I'm sorry to say it, but Susan's mother was right. He was hungry.'

'She's a bitch.'

'But sexy, don't you think? Unlike Susan.'

'Susan's sexy.'

'Not as sexy as you.'

'Jesus, Richard, why are we having such a crap conversation at this time of the morning?'

'I don't know. I find it hard to know what to say to you.'

I put croissants on to plates, find some raspberry jam in the cupboard, cut bread and get a clean pale slab of butter out of the fridge.

'It's nice watching you,' says Richard. 'You ran off last night.'

'You were pushing me.'

I watch his hand holding the bottle, his broad thumb under the nipple. I love how experienced he looks.

'Were you watching me from the window this morning, when I drove off?'

'No.'

'I thought someone was.'

'Might have been Isabel. She didn't sleep, that's why I'm giving Ant here his bottles.'

Ant. He says it with casual affection, as if for the first time the baby's a real person to him. And then he smiles down at the baby and says, 'You're doing all right on this stuff, aren't you?'

'I'll take him,' I say, and hold out my arms. 'You can make the coffee.'

Richard lifts the drowsy, wobbling baby. I take him, putting two fingers to support his neck. A burp of milk runs out of his mouth and he sneezes, and then falls asleep, hanging from my hands like a kitten. I ease him into the crook of my arm and stare down at him as Richard moves around the kitchen, taking mugs off hooks and filling the kettle. How light he is. How easy it would be to hurt him. But is being afraid of how easy it would be the same thing as wanting to do it? Layers of wanting and not wanting look into themselves like mirrors. I don't want to hurt him, but I'm afraid of wanting to hurt him. Just one finger over his nostrils would do it. And there's his pulse, bumping away in the tender centre of his head. It makes me dizzy to think how easy it would be to hurt him. He is curled in on himself, trusting the world to hold him because he has no other choice. I think of the children in the orphanage in Romania, reaching out for their drums and tambourines. They have no choice either. If any light shines, they have to turn towards it. But there's an instinct, surely there's an instinct that keeps us from doing a baby harm? Children burn with jealousy but they don't do anything. Even a jealous, raging four-year-old can tell the difference between her brother and a doll. I was a child and innocent. I never cut worms in half, or stamped on flies.

But my dolls were always alive to me. They had moods and dreams. They could be hurt and then comforted. That was the magic power we had, me and Isabel. We were their parents and we were omnipotent. I've put out of my mind some of those games we played.

'Richard.'

'What?'

'Do you ever feel frightened, you know, when you're holding him – in case you drop him?'

'All the time. I'm glad to hear women do as well.'

'But you get used to it.'

'It doesn't take long, does it? Look at you.'

I look at myself. A young woman in her sister's kitchen, holding her baby nephew while her brother-in-law makes coffee. The baby sleeps peacefully and the young woman's fingers curl protectively around his head.

'They're tougher than you think, anyway,' says Richard. 'Isabel dropped him once and it didn't seem to do much harm.'

'God, did she really? When was that?' I feel curiously relieved. If even Isabel –

'Just after she got back from hospital. She was very shaky. I came in and there he was on the floor with poor Isabel on the floor too trying to pick him up. She was in a terrible state.'

He planks a mug of coffee down in front of me.

'Don't put it there, Richard.'

'It's OK. He can't grab stuff yet.'

'I just keep thinking of things like the coffee spilling on his head.'

'It won't.' But he moves the mug. 'What you're afraid of never happens,' he says. 'It's the things you don't think of that happen.' Then he comes round behind me, pulls my head back, lets his fingers slide round my cheek, my jaw, my throat. He finds textures in me that were never there before.

'Are you going out later?'

'Yes.'

'Where?'

'The river.'

'I'll get you a croissant. Stay there.'

I eat it with my eyes shut: the jam, the cold, salty butter, the warm dissolving layers of pastry. He feeds it into my mouth inch by inch and I eat it down to the crisp, burnt point.

'I'll come,' he says. 'What time?'

'About three.'

'You'll be there.'

'Of course I will.'

You don't know who you're talking to, I think.

Chapter Nineteen

There is a way out to the water-meadows through the garden. It's a little door cut into the side wall, covered with creepers. Hard to see if you're not looking. It isn't locked, and outside there are planks laid over what would be boggy ground in any summer but this. No water now, only pale, dry grass. I shut the door behind me, the door Isabel didn't find the first time she came to her garden. Edward's gone to London for the day. I should be there too, but I'm not going. I had two calls this morning about the Romanian job, one to fix dates, the other to sort out a meeting as soon as possible. I wanted to go. While I was talking into the phone I felt like a different person, quick and definite, someone who knew how to think her way around a project as well as how to take the pictures and do the drawings. They need to meet me soon. I have to plan how I'll respond to what's going on before it's all happening in front of me in a foreign language.

I've put them off, even though I could hear seeds of doubt about me lodge as I talked. Maybe they hadn't made such a good choice after all. I told them how ill my sister is, how young the baby is and that a nanny's coming in from next week. Even while I was lying it was still nice to hear voices from that other world, with other phones ringing in the background and the tap of our conversation being noted into a word processor while it was going on. I heard the impatience of people who aren't much interested in personal things. I didn't much like it but I knew it, I felt at home with it. That's what I'll go back to, when this is over.

Isabel is the same to me as ever today, as she said she would be. She's said nothing. I made a green salad with the pizza for lunch, and put the cream doughnuts in the fridge for later. Isabel smoked cigarette after cigarette all morning, wandering around the house with a mug of coffee in her other hand. She didn't seem to know what to do without Edward.

'You shouldn't drink so much of that stuff,' I said. She buys cheap powdered coffee from the village shop, in white tins without a name on them.

'It's OK. I've stopped feeding the baby,' she said, as if the only thing that mattered was what went into the baby's milk. It's a sharp, sudden change. Isabel's cast him off. She doesn't want to give him his bottle, and Susan's spent most of the morning feeding him, winding him, feeding him again. The new milk hurts his stomach. He cries and belches, then cries while yellow streams of sick flow down his Babygros. The air is full of to-bacco smoke and screaming. Richard watches Isabel as she taps out her ash, frowning, listens for the baby, walks on. Her breasts are big and full and hurting. She keeps saying she wants the doctor to give her something to stop the milk. Richard's face is so heavy with trouble that I want to shout at him, 'For God's sake, don't let her see you looking like that.'

It's good to shut the door on it and be out. The meadows are cracked with drought, and there are bald patches where the cattle have trampled away the grass. There are hundreds of tiny pale blue butterflies, more than there've ever been, Susan says, a plague of butterflies. They don't fly, they vibrate in the heat. It's hotter now than it was at noon. You can't imagine anything else but this, day after day going on and on without cloud or breeze. The heat builds its own silence. It cuts us off as surely as a flood. Walking through the field I feel like a dot in so much summer. The trees look as if they've been suspended, let down through the air on invisible strings. Crickets chirr as I walk down the field, so fiercely that it becomes another landscape, not England. The fields are white and cracked, the sky a sharp, de-manding blue. From here you can't see the river, but when I've crossed two more fields I'll be there. Which way will Richard come? He can't cross the fields, because anyone could see him from the house. They can see me now, if they want to. Isabel can, or Susan. I've bought a larger sketchbook, and it's wedged under my arm where anyone can see it. A big, portable excuse for everything. They can see me now. Nina, full of pizza, plodding over the water-meadows. It takes her for ever. My back braces itself and a trickle of sweat gathers between my shoulders and runs slowly down my back. The cattle are bunched up by the hedge, in what shade there is.

I reach the water. It's not what I wanted. It isn't cool, or brown, or alive with fish and shadows. It is a strange porcelain green with a thick current down the middle, and a few clumps of willow and alder gripping tight to its banks. There is hardly any shade here either. Heat bounces off the water into my eyes. The towpath is narrow and because the river is slightly above the level of the meadows there is an uneasy feeling that everything has got into the wrong place. I stand and watch the water bulging round the reeds on its way downstream. It hasn't got far to go now, only five miles to the sea. It's packed with chemicals, effluent, the run-off from miles of farmland. The quality of the water is better than it was, Richard says, but no one paddles or swims here now. No one comes here, much. What is there but a high, exposed path along the snakes of the river? It bends like a river in a child's storybook, not a real river. I can't see the bottom. I remember Richard saying once, 'It's deep. Be careful, those banks are chalk and they crumble. The current's stronger than it looks.' I stare into the water. I would not want to choke in that soup of chemicals. The water doesn't smell, exactly, but it gives off a strange, metallic tang. I look up and down the banks but for miles there's nowhere hidden, nowhere we can tuck ourselves away out of sight and fuck ourselves insensible.

I sit down carefully, folding my legs under me. I watch a twig sail down the current, surprisingly fast. I open my sketchbook and take out my pencil, though there's nothing here I want to draw. Except perhaps those willow roots, the hunch and clench of them, like hands digging into soil. I move a little, turn the book round, squeeze my eyes to filter out glare.

I draw for a long time. In the middle of the drawing I realize without needing to think about it that I've stopped expecting Richard to come. Good. I'm fighting the temptation to make these roots more than roots, to turn them into the hands they aren't. Roots work differently. I rip off a sheet of spoiled paper, and I'm about to crumple it into a ball and shove it in my pocket when I have a better idea. I smooth out the paper and fold it. One fold, a turn, another fold. A triangle. A cocked hat. A little boat.

I daren't go down the white, crumbling bank. I throw the boat out. Too heavy to flutter, it turns in the air and then, amazingly, it rights itself, falls on the water and begins to sail. A current whips it from underneath and it spins, then straightens, and sails on fast down the centre of the river. I watch it until it disappears round the next bend, out of sight before it can become waterlogged and sink.

I'm still staring after it when there's a huge disturbance behind me. I think of great sheets of paper being ripped in the sky. I turn. Something big and baggy-winged stretches itself up from the river behind the next clump of willows. It hauls itself up into the air, hardly gaining any height. Like a dream of flying when you will yourself over hedges, it goes over me low, so low I duck and find myself on hands and knees on the path. And then it picks up speed with great flaps of its wings. Slowly, more slowly than I'd ever thought a bird could rise, it climbs the sky. It shows with its broad ragged wings what hard work flying is. All this time I'm holding my breath because it nearly doesn't work.

'A heron! Did you see it?' shouts Richard from across the

meadow. He's coming straight down, the way I came, so anyone can see him coming. He strides up, wiping sweat from his face. 'Did you see that! There must be fish in the river after all.'

'I can't believe that,' I say, looking into its poisonous green depths.

'Jesus, it's hot.' He looks around, as I've done, registers the lack of shade and shelter, as I've done. The walk's been too much for him. I see suddenly and coolly how much the weight and age he carries slow him down. He sits heavily beside me, and though I want to go on drawing I put down my pencil. It is much too hot for me to want to touch him. I think he must feel the same.

'Sometimes I think this place is the arse end of nowhere,' says Richard.

'I know what you mean.'

'But Isabel loves it.'

We stare out past the polluted water to the baking meadows opposite.

'This is hell,' says Richard. 'Let's walk. It can't be worse than sitting here.'

We walk one behind the other to the bend in the river. Ahead of us there are more bends, winding away to the sea between flat meadows. On the far right there's a concrete building that looks like an electricity substation. In the distance the Downs bake, almost hidden by heat haze.

'Do you want to walk on?'

'Not really.'

He laughs. 'This is awful, isn't it? What are we doing here?'

'I was drawing.'

'But it's better than being in the house,' says Richard. I look at him. This sounds like the most intimate thing he's ever said to me.

'How are things back there?'

'Isabel's missing Edward.'

'He's only been gone four hours.'

'I know. But she needs someone to talk to. She isn't feeling too good at the moment.'

We let pass, silently, the fact that she talks to neither of us.

'And Susan's buggered off to help her mother with this Young Farmers' do.'

'What?'

'I said Susan's gone over to the farm. Why, what's the matter?'

'You mean now? She's there now? She's not with Isabel?'

I've swung round to face Richard. My hands are on his elbows, gripping them. 'You mean Isabel's on her own?'

'Susan's only over at the farm. She'll be back by five. And Isabel's got the baby, so she's not really on her own.'

'The baby's with Isabel?'

'Nina, for God's sake, of course the baby's with Isabel. *What's the matter with you?*'

The heat pours on my head.

'When did Susan go?'

'I don't know, the same time as me. Yes, I saw her leave. Nina, what is all this? Isabel's fine. I wouldn't have left her if she wasn't. Nina! Where're you going?'

I scramble down the bank and into the meadow.

'Nina!'

'She shouldn't be left on her own! It's too soon!' I shout back. There are three fields and the garden between me and Isabel. I begin to run.

I am faster than Richard. I glance back and see him coming after me, thumping the dry ground, but I run faster. I've got to get there first, before anyone else sees. My feet slide on their own sweat inside my sandals. I am gasping, but I know I can run much farther than this. I climb the first stile, and drop back on to the path. The quickest way is straight across the fields. If she looks through the window, if she sees me coming, running over the fields like this, then she'll wait. She'll stand there watching, distracted, wondering what's going on. I shoot up one arm and wave madly to an invisible Isabel. *I'm coming! Stay there, don't move. Don't do anything.*

I bang the little door open. The garden's silent, stewing in heat and scent. Up the paths, hedges whipping my legs and round the side and into the stale, dark kitchen. No one there. The back door open, the clock ticking. Down the passage, across the hall, up the stairs in silent, hungry bounds. She's there. She must be. I stand and listen, but I can't hear anything. The house is as quiet as if everyone's stopped breathing. Then I hear her singing. Her nice voice, thin but sweet:

> *'My daddy was a preacher*
> *my daddy was a thief*
> *eevy ivy overhead*
> *how many hours does the baby sleep*
> *eevy ivy overhead . . .'*

I know it well. That song's lodged in my bones, like all the songs Isabel once sang me. She begins again

> *'My daddy was a preacher . . .'*

and all those summer evenings of Isabel's singing tumble back over me. I take in a breath. I am hot, shivering with heat. I hear Isabel stir inside the room, the chair creak, her footsteps light on the bare boards –

I open the door. The cot's empty.

'Where's the baby?'

'The baby?' Isabel opens her eyes wide. I see the fringe of her lashes spray wide. Her eyes are clear as storybook rivers. 'He's in

Susan's room of course. Fast asleep. For heaven's sake don't go in and wake him up. It took me forever to get him off.'

'Oh. I thought you were singing to him.'

'I wasn't singing.'

'You were. I heard you.'

'What then? What was I singing?'

I purse my lips. I hate singing, even when I'm alone. Isabel could sing, I couldn't. 'You were singing

'How many hours does the baby sleep.'

Isabel laughs. 'I haven't thought of that for years, Neen.' Her tense face is relaxing, slowly. 'But where've you been?'

'Down by the river,' I say quickly. 'I was drawing.'

'I know. I saw you go.'

'Did you see Richard too? He came down thinking it would be cooler, but it was even hotter by the river.'

'Yes, I saw him.' She turns aside, pulling at her dress. 'Christ, look at this. I'm soaked in milk again.'

'It'll stop soon, won't it?'

'Susan says so. She'd know, of course.'

'Of course.' Our eyes meet in shared amusement.

'Why doesn't she have one,' demands Isabel, 'why doesn't she just bloody well have one?'

'The same reason I don't,' I say; 'she doesn't want one.'

'You do, Neen, of course you do,' croons Isabel, dabbing milk off herself.

'I'm going to make some tea. There are those cream dough-nuts in the fridge. Do you want any?'

Isabel glances up, her eyes sliding past mine. 'Look in on the baby for me, Neen, on your way down. Just to check he's all right.'

The sweat from my run chills all over me. I'm tangled up as I was in her singing, tangled up in words I've heard before, in things that have happened once and should never happen again.

Surely she knows what she's saying. Careless and intimate, that's how we look. Two sisters in a bedroom. *On your way down . . . just to check he's all right . . . go and look at the baby, Neen. Go and look at the baby.*

Chapter Twenty

Slowly, slowly, I push open the door of Susan's room. I make no sound. The pale curtains are drawn, and the room smells of the new pine furniture and baby sleep. He is rosy with the heat, his hair damp, his fist up to his face. He is sleeping on his side and Isabel has put a rolled-up towel beside him so that he can't turn on to his face. I creep right up to the cot. His weight dents the mattress. He looks more solid than I've ever seen him. Already he's changing, filling out, and that fist by his face looks strangely mature. He is sleeping peacefully in the thick yellow light which filters through Susan's curtains. All my fears sink down. He's well, perfectly well. I've been imagining things.

Richard is at the bottom of the stairs, looking up.

'What was all that about? I couldn't keep up with you.'

But he hasn't tried. He must have been waiting down there for a while, because he's not out of breath any more. I wonder why he didn't come up after me. Perhaps he didn't want to break in on me and Isabel, but I doubt it. 'She's a lot tougher than you think, you know,' he says.

'I got worried about her being alone in the house. It was stupid.'

I stand on the bottom stair, and our eyes are almost on a level.

'You think of her more than she thinks of you,' said Richard.

'I don't know how you can think that.'

'Because I see things from the outside.'

'You're wrong. Isabel's always been—' But it's hard to find words for what Isabel's always been.

'I think you need to get away from Isabel.' He's entirely serious.

'How can you say that? She's my sister, she's always looked after me.'

'Has she?'

'Richard, how can you talk like this about Isabel? You're married to her. She's my sister.'

'It's got nothing to do with how I feel about Isabel. I know her very, very well. I know her much better than you do. I don't think you two do each other any good. Isabel knows what she wants, Nina.'

'And I don't?'

'No. You don't let yourself. You're in a dream half the time.'

It's the economist talking, the fulfilment man. The lens is on me and it's going to come zooming in. I start to gabble out a diversion. 'I'm going to make some tea to take up to Isabel. The baby's asleep so she's going to rest till he wakes up.'

In the kitchen I make myself quick and busy, filling a tray with milk and mugs and plates. I take three doughnuts out of the fridge.

'Do you want one?'

'Why are you giving that to Isabel? She won't want it.'

I lay Isabel's doughnut on a plate on the tray. It is puffy and light, covered with white and brown scribbles of icing.

'I'll eat it,' says Richard, stretching out his hand.

'I bought enough for one each. That one in the bag's yours.'

'But you know she doesn't –'

'She might.'

The kettle boils and I pour water into the pot. Richard puts his hand on the back of my knee. 'Shit, Richard, this is boiling water.'

'I know. But you've got steady hands, I've watched you.' He slides his hand up, over my thigh, inside the cuff of my shorts. I put down the kettle with my steady hands but I don't turn. 'I'll come down,' I say. 'I won't be long. I'll just take this up to Isabel.'

'She doesn't sleep with me any more, you know,' says Richard.

'Of course she does. She got pregnant with Antony.'

'That didn't take long. She'd got it worked it out so it only took one go.'

'You don't need to tell me any of that. I don't care.'

'Because it's separate? That's the way you see it?'

'I don't see it any way.'

'No, you don't, do you? We don't have to think and we don't have to talk. Everything goes on in the dark. Well, that may be fine for you, but it isn't for me.'

'Take your hand away if you don't like it.'

His hand tightens on my thigh. 'I'd love you to stand there naked, cooking,' he says.

'With maybe a little apron?'

'I'm not that perverse.'

'What would I cook?'

'I don't know. Anything. You'd be there chopping and stirring. Tasting things. You always taste when you cook, don't you?'

'I can't cook any other way.'

'You'd have a wooden spoon in your mouth.'

'And you'd watch.'

'Oh no, I'd do more than that.'

'Food's important. You don't want to go mixing it up with other things.'

'You would, though, wouldn't you? You would, wouldn't you?'

Isabel's tray is cheap and buckled. The teapot slips, but I balance it and push her door open with my knee.

'Oh Neen, tea, lovely. Let me shove all this stuff off the table.' She's been writing another letter. I pull up the other chair, and sit down opposite her.

'You don't still take sugar in tea, do you, Neen? It's bad for your skin.'

'I need it after all that running.'

'I saw you. What on earth was the matter? You tearing up the field and Richard chasing you. It looked as if he'd been trying it on down by the river.' She laughs.

'You know, Isabel, how you said we weren't going to talk about last night – about what we talked about last night?'

'We're not,' she answers quickly. 'I said I wouldn't talk about it again and I won't.' This time it sounds like a declaration, not a reassurance.

'I want to. I've been thinking about it all night.' I lean forward and begin to divide the two doughnuts into eight quarters with a sharp knife. I cut them very carefully so that the dough isn't squashed down on the cream. Isabel feels on her table for the cigarette pack, taps one out without looking and lights it. I know how Isabel smokes when there's food around, so that the cigarette makes a barrier between her and the plate. She can't put food in her mouth if there's a cigarette in it. I pour tea for us both.

'Why do you want to?' says Isabel.

'I went in to look at Ant just now. He was asleep. He looked so –'

'Peaceful.'

'No. That's not the right word. I don't know how to describe it. He looked *there*. Solid. A hundred per cent alive. And I thought, Colin must have looked like that. He's been dead such a long time I've been thinking of him as if he was never really alive. But he was. He was solid too.'

Isabel draws sharply on her cigarette. 'So?'

'And when I started to think about it, I couldn't believe that even when I was only four years old, I wouldn't have felt the difference. Between what you can do to a doll and what you can do to a baby.'

'But Colin died.' I watch the tidemark of milk on her dress, moving with her quick breath.

'Yes. But maybe it wasn't that way.'

'I saw it. I know it was. I was seven, remember.'

'It could have been an accident.'

A breath goes out of Isabel, and her shoulders sink. She looks down, at the end of her cigarette, and then up. 'I suppose . . . I suppose it could have been.' She frowns, thinking back. There's a little more colour in her face now.

'I would have remembered killing him,' I say. The words erupt in the room like vomit, and Isabel flinches. 'Don't say that.'

'But that's what it means, doesn't it, if it wasn't an accident? It means I killed him. What else could have happened?'

'That's why you ran back,' says Isabel. 'You thought, if it could happen to Colin for no reason then it could happen to Antony. Isn't that what it was? You were frightened. You were out of breath when you came in.'

I look at her. Again Isabel's taken what's happened and made it a different truth that I can't argue with. 'Yes, I suppose it was.'

'But I'm sure I saw what I saw,' Isabel goes on, frowning more deeply.

'It's not just what you see, though, is it? It's what you make of what you see. You have to interpret things.'

And then it comes to me. I don't just see it, I see and I know. Colin's legs were moving. Bare, purple, weak legs beating up and down on the mattress as Isabel bent over the cot. *I saw that.* Could I have made it up? Made myself see movement where there was only stillness? Could I have been so terrified of what I'd done that I not only hid it from myself for ever, but made up another scene, one where Isabel stood over the baby and the baby was alive, half-hidden by her body, struggling? Have I made those pictures in my mind, frame by frame? Isabel stood by the cot while I watched from the door. And she leaned down, pressed down.

I could have invented it all. I might be capable of that. How am I going to find out what I'm capable of? I stare at my golden sister.

'Don't worry, Neen. Everything's all right.'

Isabel looks at me as if we've said all we need to say. I feel trapped, overwhelmed. I know nothing and I can't trust my own memory. Isabel is so sure.

'We've never been all that happy, you know,' she says.

'What?'

'Me and Richard. It's been difficult for a long time.'

I wrench my mind round to this. 'You and Richard?'

She nods, and I believe her. The mystery of Isabel and Richard used to be one of my touchstones. That was the way you could be, if you found the right person. I thought they possessed a happiness they hid to keep it safe from outsiders. They were the adults, the ones who knew how life worked.

'No, it was never much good.' She stares straight at me, shrugging off everything. 'And now I can't bear it. I can't have him near me.'

She stubs out her cigarette. 'Are those doughnuts nice, Neen?'

'They're fantastic. Really light, not greasy at all.'

Isabel hesitates. I feel her wanting, but I don't know what she wants. Was there a time once, before she'd coached herself out of hunger, that we could stand in front of the baker's shop together and point at cream slices and Eccles cakes and éclairs? Was there a time when we'd both watch jealously as the tinned pineapple was divided, piece by piece, until our bowls were exactly equal? 'Go on,' I say. 'You know you're hungry.'

Isabel stretches out her long, delicate hand. She picks up a quarter of iced doughnut, holding it as if it's a grasshopper. Her hand shakes slightly as she turns her wrist, lifts the doughnut to her mouth, takes a small bite, and chews. After a little while, effortfully, she swallows.

'Quite nice,' she says, her eyes watering.

I pick another piece for myself off the plate. 'Just as well this is the last one. I could pig out on these.'

'You're lucky,' says Isabel, 'you can eat what you want.'

We drink our tea, and in spite of everything we're more relaxed together than we've been for a long time. Isabel doesn't light any more cigarettes. Her piece of doughnut lies on the plate, the cream melting into a yellow puddle. The cuffs of her soft red shirt lie loosely on her slender wrists. She turns a ring on the little finger of her right hand, a turquoise and silver ring she bought in Kashmir, long before she met Richard. She brought me back a bracelet, made of the same turquoise, with silver links that turned black when I wore it.

'But there's the baby,' says Isabel abruptly, out of some long, private train of thought.

'That might make things better.'

'The trouble is, men need sex.'

It's such an odd thing to say, so unlike Isabel, but at the same time so truly Isabelline that I smile. Isabel flushes slightly.

'They do,' I say.

'I don't though, do you? Not really. You soon get used to not having it. I remember thinking the same about food. All those people thinking they had to have food all the time or they'd die, always thinking about it and talking about it and going out to the shops for it and then sitting chomping it down, and yet it wasn't really necessary at all. All the world turned on something you could do without. I wanted to shout out and tell everyone the truth.'

'But you didn't.'

'Oh no,' says Isabel, 'that sort of thing you keep to yourself, don't you?'

She smiles, a real, curling smile, as if we're conspirators. I remember her telling me Sunday school was shit and freeing me for ever from wanting to bow down to anything.

'You don't need to worry about Richard,' I say. 'There are plenty of other people in the world who like sex.'

'That's what I keep hoping.'

'Don't worry about it. He'll be fine.'

One word more would be too many. We hover on the edge of what can't be said, caught up, as we used to be caught in the histories we made up for Rosina and Mandy. They were always changing. That was the best thing about the dolls. If the storyline didn't work out, we could wipe out their pasts. Suddenly I remember how Isabel decided one summer that Rosina had long raven hair.

'What's raven?'

'Black.'

'But Rosina's got yellow hair.'

'That doesn't matter. It's raven now,' said Isabel, picking up the dolls' hairbrush.

'Is it?'

'Of course it is. It's part of the game. Now you say *Are you going to brush Rosina's raven hair?*'

'Are you going to brush Rosina's raven hair, Isabel?' I asked.

I squinted at the doll. On her coarse, vigorous yellow hair I thought I detected a faint sheen of black.

'As long as Richard's happy, I don't mind,' says Isabel.

'You want to stay together.'

'Yes, why not?'

'There's no reason why not.'

I go downstairs with the empty mugs and pot rattling on the tray. It's half-past five. The zone of safety is nearly over: the earliest train Edward could catch comes in at five-fifteen. But even if he gets that train, he'll have to ring for a taxi at the station, and that'll take a while to come. And then there's Susan, walking back over the fields from the farm. She shouldn't be back for a while yet.

Richard is slicing tomatoes into a bowl.

'You haven't skinned them.'

'It's not worth it.'

'It's those little touches that make all the difference.'

'I'm sure.' He puts down the knife. 'You were a long time.'

'We were just talking.'

'Do you want to go in the garden?'

'No.' Isabel's hand is on me. Her permission freezes me. 'No, I'm not —'

'I see.' He goes on slicing tomatoes, expertly, his face closed.

'You don't. You don't see anything.' I take the knife out of his hand.

Not the garden, because the garden is Isabel's place. But the kitchen, here with juice dripping off the knife and cream souring, that's my place. The door to the passage is half-open, and the back-door too. But there's nothing anywhere but the dead quiet of late afternoon. I pull my T-shirt over my head.

'What are you doing?'

'You can see what I'm doing.'

'Jesus, Nina. Isabel might come down any minute.'

'She won't.'

'And we can't lie on this floor. Look at the muck down there.'

'We'll do it standing up against the cooker.'

'Is it off?'

'Of course it's off.'

We lean together. There's no time to spare but I'm weak with slowness. I want to do everything as if it's for the first time. Unbutton each button, slide it out of its little sewn nest. Pull back his shirt. Lie against his chest, sinking into the thickness of his flesh with my heart thudding as if I'm still running over the fields. I shut my eyes.

He shoves me upright. 'Nina, get your clothes on. There's a car.'

I stoop, grab my T-shirt off the floor, pull it over my head, stand up again, dizzy. The car engine's stopped, and there are voices.

'Edward.'

We move apart. Richard sits down at the table and picks up the knife. I turn the cold tap full on in a noisy gush and put a saucepan underneath it. Water bounces up from the bare metal and spatters me. The car engine starts again and footsteps crunch, stop, crunch on again, past the kitchen door.

'He's going in through the garden.'

We look at each other, and I push back my hair with a wet hand.

'He's going to stay here till I go back to London. He won't leave us alone,' I say.

'Do you think he's guessed?'

'He knows.'

'Does he?' Richard's face is tense, focused. This is what he must look like at work, an economist working out the odds on growth in a small, unstable economy.

'But he won't say anything,' I say. 'This suits him really. He's got Isabel to himself. Hours of talk in the bedroom while we're out of the way.'

'You can't be sure of that. He'll do anything for her.'

The levels of what I'm capable of buzz and shift in my head. 'I'm going to go back to London tomorrow,' I say, as if it's long planned. I watch for the tiny shrinkage of his pupils in his still face, the sign of disappointment he can't hide.

Chapter Twenty-one

'I want us to have a celebration,' says Isabel. We all turn: Richard from the paper, Edward from the floor where he's assembling the mobile he's bought for the baby in London. I look up from spreading toast with black cherry jam. It's too hot already, and riding towards the thirty-four degrees forecast for today, although it's only half-past eight. All the windows are open. It was too hot to sleep, and the baby howled from two until four. I kept listening for rain, the way I used to listen for the sea. The ground's as hard and tight as a drum. All night I slid in and out of sleep and I woke up aching. It's oppressively close this morning. 'A celebration?'

'Yes. I couldn't sleep because it was so hot, and I've been thinking about it all night. We ought to do something, before you all go. We're never going to get a summer like this again, with all of you staying here. And Susan's leaving soon, so I thought we'd ask her and Margery as well. But not anyone else, no one from London. Just us.'

The line between Isabel's eyes has become a deep groove. She glances round at us all, her eyes very bright. If I touched Isabel now she'd spark.

'Don't you think it's a good idea?'

'What sort of celebration?' asks Richard.

I know what he means, but Isabel answers a different question. 'A dinner. We'll eat outside, on the terrace. We'll take the long table out, and hang those candle lanterns in the apple trees for when it gets dark. There's that white cloth your mother gave us, Richard, the linen one with the ivy pattern. And the triple candlestick. Candles will burn outside as well as they do indoors in this weather.'

'It'll be a lot of work for Nina,' says Richard, looking at me. 'That salmon took you most of the day, didn't it?'

'It won't be left to her,' says Isabel sharply. 'We'll all do it together. We'll each choose a dish, and cook it.'

'A family feast,' says Edward. It's impossible to tell if his tone is pleased or ironic. Against my will, I start to warm to the idea and see what it could be like. The table loaded, the cloth crowded with bottles and flowers, the blue dusk and then the candles. A feast to end everything that's happened here and set us free from one another. A feast that'll put a shape round our confusion and give it a name. But I was going to go home today, and it's so hot. My skin itches at the thought of all that shopping, and the car cooking in its own fumes on roads full of people desperate to get to the sea.

Richard goes over to the window. 'It looks like thunder,' he remarks, as if this has nothing to do with Isabel's plan.

'It won't rain. It's been like this for weeks,' says Isabel quickly. 'Look at those clouds over there.'

It looks as if someone has drawn shapes on the sky with a metallic pen. They're the faintest of outlines, gathering in the distance.

'That's nothing,' says Edward. 'It won't rain, the forecast said it'd be even hotter this afternoon. It's going to beat all the records. Do you know this is the hottest summer there's been for two hundred years?'

'We need rain,' says Richard.

'How would you know? You spend half your life up in an aeroplane,' says Isabel.

'You can see a lot from a plane.'

'So, when's this celebration going to be?' asks Edward.

'I thought we'd have it tonight. There's plenty of time, if we each work out what we're going to cook now, and then you and Richard and Nina go and do all the shopping. You'll have to go into Brighton to get everything. If you and Richard carry the table and chairs out first, then Susan can decorate them while you're out. I want flowers everywhere, and ivy, and vine-leaves. I'll look after the baby.'

'Are you sure you're up to this, Isabel? You know how tired you are,' says Richard. But Isabel is flushed, electric. 'Of course I'm all right. At least I'll be doing something instead of sitting around waiting for the baby to cry.'

'It's a fantastic idea,' says Edward, getting up. He's put together the frame of the mobile and now he reaches up to hang it from a hook on the back of the door. 'You'll have to put a hook in the ceiling for this, Isabel, over the baby's cot.'

There are dozens of blue wooden fish in the box. One by one Edward takes them out and threads them into place. The mobile is going to be a huge cage of fish.

'How many fish are there?' asks Richard.

'Forty.'

'It'll take up half the room. He won't be able to see the sky.'

'It's beautiful,' says Isabel.

'He'll grow up believing that fish can fly,' I say.

'Does that matter?'

'Of course it matters. What kind of a picture of the world is he going to have?'

'A better one than we had,' says Isabel. Her fingers play with the light dry fish. The fish we saw flopping in the bottom of fishing boats in our childhood weren't like that. They had weight, and muscle. They were slippery when you picked them up, their blood was bright, like human blood, and their eyes looked as if they were watching you. On a good day you could get a shopping bag full of herring for a shilling. We ate a lot of herring.

The mobile is a tangle of wood and thread, but Edward works his way through it confidently. We're all watching him now, the way people watch anyone who's doing something with his hands. Isabel picks up another fish. 'There,' says Edward, pointing, 'slip the thread through the little hook.' The thread is plastic, and invisible from where I am, but Isabel ties nothing to nothing, and there the fish hangs.

'That's going to take you forever,' says Susan, coming in with Antony asleep at last, his face puffed and blotched.

'It won't take long.'

Isabel and Edward work together, and I wonder if I'm the only one who sees how alike they are. I watch their slender fingers, their fine concentrated faces. They could be brother and sister. They are so much more alike than Isabel and me. Next to them I look like a peasant, and so does Richard. Richard's watching them too, as they construct the mobile for his son.

'We'll get this finished,' says Edward, 'and then we'll plan tonight. We'll have to have music. Are you well enough to dance?'

'If it's a slow number,' says Isabel.

'What's happening tonight?' asks Susan.

'There's going to be a party,' says Richard, his voice and face expressionless.

'Not a party, a celebration,' says Isabel, her mouth full of thread.

'What's the difference?'

'A party's open to anyone. This is private.'

'I'll go home for the evening, then,' says Susan stiffly.

'Oh no, Susan, I didn't mean that. You've got to come. You must come. Please. It won't be the same without you.'

Isabel stretches out her hand to Susan, pleading, and Susan melts at once. She'll come, of course she will, and so will her mother. All we have to think about now is what we're going to cook.

'Six courses,' says Isabel.

'But you can't just have six of anything. You have to plan it so the dishes work together.' It's so obvious it shouldn't have to be said.

'They're separate courses, anyway, so it doesn't really matter,' says Isabel, turning her obstinate, beautiful face towards me without really looking at me. I can't put into words how a meal should be, how there should be pauses, and tiny repetitions, reactions of taste against taste. How it should build from the first note, then die down again. Isabel won't think about any of that. She won't consider the colours and textures of food, because she doesn't want to give it that much attention. Food has been crushed down into a small space in Isabel's mind. Six courses: one for each of us except Antony. Why should anyone count Antony? But if there's going to be a celebration I can't think of anything apart from his existence that we can possibly be celebrating. I could make a cake and ice his name on it.

No one's asked why Isabel wants a feast, when she won't eat anything at it. This house is stiff with things which can't be said. When we're all in the same room what we say sounds more like code than conversation. But who wrote the code? Who's forcing us to use it?

'When are you leaving, Nina?' asks Richard in front of everyone.

'I was thinking of going today, but I'll wait till tomorrow now.'

'I'll miss you, Neen,' says Isabel, with a quick, public smile. 'It's been lovely having you here for so long.'

She's very tense. She pulls a plastic thread too hard and it snaps, but Edward ties it up in an invisible knot and it's all right. Isabel sits back on her heels, blinking and wiping her hands, which are wet with sweat. 'I can't do it, Edward,' she says in a voice blank with distress. Then, visibly, she gathers herself together. 'It's hurting my eyes. Nina, have you thought of what you're going to do for the meal yet?'

I haven't thought at all, but I don't need to. 'Figs,' I say.

'Figs?'

'Yes. Black Turkish figs. They're just coming into season. I saw some the other day. A huge plate of fresh figs so we can have as many as we want for once. We could eat them at the beginning of the meal, or at the end. They won't spoil the taste of whatever comes next. I'll whip some cream to go with them, though I think they're better without.'

'You're not going to cook, then?'

'Isabel, they'll be perfect, I promise you. Better than anything I could cook. I'll probably make something else as well, but that's a surprise.'

'Oh!' She relaxes. 'You *are* cooking something, then.'

The figs mean nothing to her. Their white paper packing, the fragile bloomy skin of each fruit, the way the seeds ooze slowly through cracks in the flesh, the fleshy fatness at the base of the stem. I bought figs in Dubrovnik market once, before it was shelled. The market women laid them out on leaves and when you looked closely you could see tiny fissures, like a crazy paving of sweetness, because the fruit was ripe to bursting. I ate figs and oranges with black coffee every morning and I found out that figs are never one colour. They're black, then purple, but they always have some green left in them too, and as the skin grows thinner you see the brown-gold of flesh through it.

I see Richard swallow.

'What about all of you?'

'I'll make a fish soup,' Edward says. 'If we're going into Brighton I know a good fishmonger there. Shrimp and garlic soup with coriander. It's the fish stock that takes the time.'

Fish stock is easy, as we both know, but Edward is scoring points this morning. 'Or there's a Galician fish stew I've been wanting to try out,' he muses, 'but you have to boil up olive oil and water to cook the fish and the timing's tricky – if the emulsion's not right the fish boils to rags –'

'Make the soup.'

'I know what I can bring,' says Susan. 'My mum's got an ice-cream maker, and she's made boxes and boxes for the Young

Farmers – it's all in the freezer. There's gooseberry crumble ice-cream, and butterscotch, and raspberry. I'll put one of each in a freezer pack and bring it over.'

'I thought I'd make a fruit salad,' says Isabel.

Now there's a tradition of my mother's that Isabel has kept up. A sodden mass of tinned peaches and cocktail cherries in colourless syrup, brought to life by a quarter pound of green grapes and a couple of oranges hacked into slices. If my mother was feeling reckless she would tip in a glass of brandy to add smoulder to the tang of metal and sugar. Always cheap brandy. She could never really stop being careful. But Isabel isn't doing the shopping, and I think I can remember a recipe for mango and peach slices with fresh lime and ginger syrup.

'Do you mind what fruit we get, or shall we just buy whatever looks good?'

'Oh anything,' says Isabel. 'I've got loads of tins. I think I've even got a tin of lychees somewhere.'

'That seems to leave me with the main course,' says Richard.

'I know what you can do. It'll fit in with everything perfectly, and it isn't difficult,' I say. 'Roasted vegetables with couscous in layers with goat's cheese. We'll do aubergines and red peppers and courgettes and little onions. It sounds a mess but it's good. You could do tabbouleh as a side dish, and goat's cheese in filo pastry parcels.'

'Christ, Nina.'

Isabel laughs. 'There you are, Richard.'

'OK. This is what you've got to do. Don't cook the couscous, let it soak for ten minutes in boiling stock. That works better. There's stock in the fridge, and you can chop a couple of leaves of mint into it after you've boiled it up, and then strain it again. You only want an edge of mint in the couscous. The peppers need to be seared. If they're sweet enough you'll get that black, sticky taste from the skin, almost a toffee taste. And that'll bring out the sweetness in the onions too. All the other stuff's easy:

we'll buy the filo pastry from the Greek shop and the cheese too. It's always fresh there. And those fat squashy olives.'

'Easy,' says Richard.

'It's OK, I'll help you. Let me just write down olive oil. That stuff I bought in the village is no good. And bread,' I write on the back of an envelope. 'Cheese. Champagne. How many bottles? I'm paying.'

'No, you're not,' says Richard quickly. 'You're not paying for anything this time, Nina.'

'So put your purse away,' says Isabel.

We smile. We smile like sisters, like what we should be instead of what we are. For a second Edward's the family friend who's splashed out on an expensive toy for the baby to whom he'll be unofficial uncle. Richard is the proud father going out to buy champagne to wet the head of his first son. Isabel is the young mother who's had a bad time but is getting back on her feet now. And I'm the aunt, the sister-in-law, the sister, the friend. The cook. Whatever you want.

'There,' says Edward, 'that's done.' Carefully, he unhooks the finished mobile from the back of the door. He holds the frame where the two pieces of wood cross, and gives it a small shake. The fish shiver into position. The wires bounce a little, the threads go up and down, the fish wince and then start to swim through the air. Isabel claps her hands.

'It's wonderful, Edward. I never thought it would be so beautiful.'

There's too much emotion in her voice again, as there was when she pleaded with Susan, but Edward doesn't seem to notice. He smiles as he pushes the mobile again with one finger and all the fishes turn. There's a tiny clacking sound as their wooden fins touch. Edward's face is proud and absorbed.

'Antony's going to love this,' he says, as if Antony's a person with tastes of his own.

'So we're going into town,' says Richard, standing up. 'We'd better finish that list.'

'It doesn't need all three of us to go. I'll stay with you, Isabel,' says Edward. But Isabel leans back in her chair and shuts her eyes. 'You go. You need to get all the stuff for your fish soup.'

'I can write it all down for them, and stay with you. You don't want to be on your own.'

'I shan't be on my own, I've got Susan. Really, Edward, I'd much rather you went. You've been stuck in with me since you got here. You could all have lunch out together, and I'll sleep for a couple of hours or I'll be dead later on. Susan'll do the table, and then she can mind Antony, can't you, Susan?'

'If you're tired, the baby can always come out with me while I do the table as well. He's no trouble. And I'll ring Mum, shall I, about tonight?'

'I'll ring her,' says Isabel.

'We'll get that table moved then, Edward,' says Richard. Even the way he says it sounds grim and masculine. They get up, facing one another, two men who don't like one another but are used to having to get on. Now that they're face to face I realize just how much they dislike one another. Their bodies know it. They move into position like boxers, and there are patches of sweat under Richard's arms already, before they've even started lifting. They go out together.

'What flowers shall I pick?' asks Susan.

'Whatever you like,' says Isabel. 'Pick everything.'

She says it carelessly and Susan nods, because she has no way of knowing that this is something Isabel could never possibly mean. She doesn't like picking any flowers for the house at all, though she gives way grudgingly and puts a few roses on the table when people are coming. Isabel would know if two heads of white phlox were cut from her border. She knows which rose is ready to drop its petals at a touch.

'Cut the black dahlias. And the Japanese anemones have come out early because of the heat. They'd look good with the dahlias,' she tells Susan. The black dahlias are rare. I've never seen their tiny velvet flowers in any other garden. They have bronze leaves, and Isabel has planted them in a mass in front of a sage bush. They are never cut for the house.

'Where are those, then?' asks Susan.

'Go down past the cherry tree; they're in the bed on your left, by the wall. No, never mind, I'll cut them for you. But take anything else you want from the garden, Susan. Cut what you like,' repeats Isabel, her veiled, cloudy eyes turned in my direction. Her hand dangles by the spread quilt where Susan has laid the baby. She does not quite touch him, but an inch closer and her fingers would brush his lips.

Chapter Twenty-two

I follow Isabel out into the garden. She walks ahead of me easily, swinging secateurs from her right hand. Her brown-skinned arms are silky in the morning light. I want to slow her down, to draw all the beautiful retreating triangles of her walk down the path. You'd never think she had been afraid of anything. She brushes under the low branch of an apple tree and holds it up, waiting for me.

'Are you following me?'

'No, I'm just –'

'I'm quite all right. There's nothing the matter with me at all.' She looks up at the sky. 'There won't be a storm; look at that blue.'

The path is covered with flying ants, crawling and dragging their wings. It looks as if a nest has been kicked open.

'Why don't they fly?'

'They will later on. It's like the anemones, everything's coming out too early. And look at these apples.' She taps the branch sharply and five or six immature fruit bounce on to the path.

'I can't help stepping on them.'

The ants disgust me. Their long, fly-like bodies seem fit for nothing, neither walking nor flight.

'I'll bring out a kettle of boiling water later and pour it over the nest, or we'll have them crawling up to the house,' says Isabel.

'You aren't really going to cut those dahlias, are you?'

'Why not? They'll look wonderful in a tall vase with the anemones. There are enough to fill three or four vases, all down the table.' She walks on, past the cherry tree, and there's the sage

144

bush, its purple flowers heavy with bees, with the soft black dahlias in front of it.

'I've never known these come out so early,' says Isabel. She stands on the path contemplating the mass of flowers.

'Don't pick them. They look so lovely.'

'Were you thinking of drawing them?'

'I should. They're beautiful.'

'You won't,' says Isabel. 'You won't get round to it. You've got other things to do.' She unclips the secateurs, leans forward and begins to slice off flower stems. At first she cuts long stems, but instead of gathering them she lets them fall to the ground. Some of them get trapped on the way down so that she slices through the same stem twice. They fall and catch on one another. I bend and try to pick them up.

'Careful. I'm still cutting.' I snatch my fingers back as Isabel's steel secateurs shut on another tall bronze stem. 'There,' she says, 'that should be enough.' But the flowers are so profuse that there are still dozens left. Isabel shoves the cut dahlias aside with her foot, so that she can get closer to the plant. Leaning closer into it, she begins to snip off each tiny head with quick, short squeezes on the secateurs.

'Don't! Don't, Isabel.' But she carries on. Dahlia heads drop to the dry soil and the path like velvet buttons. Snip, snip, snip, snip. Soon the big branching dahlia plant is shorn of its flowers.

'There,' says Isabel. She is slightly out of breath. She stands, exhausted, the secateurs dangling at her side. The sun burns, as if through a metal mesh. There's a buzz in the air and I think of insects, then thunder, but then we both look up at once and there's the plane, its long black and silver pennant streaming behind it. It has the moon stitched on it, and the stars.

'Come to Damiano's Dreamworld,' it says, louder and louder as the plane comes over us lower than it's ever done before.

'He's wasting his time,' says Isabel. 'No one's going from here.'

The engine drone drifts and stutters. The plane picks up a little height and goes off across the water-meadows, taking its message with it.

'Why did you do that?' I ask Isabel, touching the flowers with my toe.

'Susan'll have plenty for her arrangements.' Isabel stoops to gather the long stems. 'Hadn't you better get going? Richard and Edward are waiting for you.'

'Izzy, what's the matter?' Her face is empty, her shoulders bowed. She looks as if she's acting the part of an old woman. 'I don't want to leave you.'

'There is nothing wrong with me, Nina.' She spits out the words in controlled syllables.

'I know there is. Don't be like this with me. It's me, Neen. Your sister. I only want you to –'

Isabel rubs a hand over her face, to and fro, pressing so hard I see the flesh whiten round her fingers. When she speaks it's as if she's wiped away herself to let out a new voice. Or perhaps an old one. It echoes like something I've heard before, and know well. It's a high, sweet voice that makes the hairs rise on my arms. A child's voice. 'Is that what you want, Neen? All right. I promise.' I stare at her and the voice trickles into the silence. I'm not sure she even knows I'm still here. Then she looks down, focuses on the secateurs and then up at me. She's herself again. 'I'm so tired, you don't know how tired I am. Just let me get some sleep today and I'll be fine tonight.'

I lick my lips. 'You go to bed, Iz. I'll tell Susan you need to rest and she'll look after the baby for you. Listen, why are we doing all this with the meal anyway? Nobody'd mind if –'

'I want to do it.' She has a faint smile on her face and she looks overwhelmingly like my father. For a second I can hardly see Isabel at all; it's like looking at her through the body of a ghost.

'It's OK,' she says, 'I'll tell Susan. Quick, you'd better go.

They'll be in the car. You know what they get like if they have to wait.'

Isabel and I both smile weakly, and then Isabel bends to pick up more flowers. She scrabbles together a double handful of buttons that are already losing their sheen. Half of them drop back on the path. Each time she handles the flowers they look worse.

'What am I going to do with them?' she asks me.

'Leave them. Chuck them away. For Christ's sake, Iz, it's not a crime to pick flowers. They're only a bush of sodding dahlias, even if you did grow them. *It doesn't matter.*'

She nods. Her hands droop at her sides with the dahlia heads spilling out of them.

'Susan can pick something else,' I say. And she leaves them. I think I see relief in her face. We don't touch, we don't say goodbye. I watch her walk slowly back up the path to the house.

Chapter Twenty-three

Brighton is swarming.

'We should have gone out-of-town, to the shopping centre,' says Richard.

This is the third time we've cruised this block, waiting for someone to move. We've already spotted the tow-away truck six cars in front of us, with someone's Audi in its jaws.

'Oh, you sweetheart,' croons Richard, as a burly man in his sixties reverses his well-polished Honda out of a space. 'Have you got the parking card ready, Neen?' I scratch off the date and the time, and put the ticket in the window. 'We'll be quicker if we work separately,' says Richard briskly. 'Your fish shop's down there, Edward, turn left, across the road and second right with the pub on the corner.'

'I know.'

'You'll be how long? An hour?'

'About that. And you'll be shopping together.'

'We'll have to. Nina's the only one who knows what to get for this dish I'm supposed to be cooking.'

I sit in the mother seat, the power seat, and watch Edward walk away, swinging his string bag.

'Jesus, it's even hotter here. Have we really got to do this shopping or can we go to a pub?'

'We can go to a pub if we cheat and buy the whole lot at Waitrose while Edward's traipsing round looking for fresh coriander.'

'There's a good one just down here.'

The sea's like a wall at the end of the street, oily and still. The pub's got a couple of tables out on the narrow, glaring pavement. Eight chairs are packed round each table and there's a reek of sun-oil and beer.

'Let's go inside.'

It's dark inside, and half-empty. The back-door's open to let some air through, and it shows the corner of a blindingly white yard where there are a couple of umbrellas and tables. But it's better to be indoors. An old man on the far side looks up without curiosity, and then back into his pint, as we pick a table in the corner.

Richard slides into the bench next to me. 'I hope the gin doesn't give you a headache.'

'I've got one already. It'll take it away.'

I lean back and feel the gin begin to move through me. On an empty stomach it's dazzling. I move up close to Richard so our thighs touch, then press.

'I could fuck you here on this bench,' he says.

'And here we are with half an hour and there's nowhere to go.'

He laughs. 'I shouldn't think anyone's ever said that in Brighton before. Walk out of here and we'd pass ten hotels in a hundred yards.'

'Edward might get fed up waiting.'

'Bugger Edward. Anyway, you said he knows.'

But we both know nothing's going to happen here.

'They'd do a good trade renting out beach-huts by the hour, come to think of it,' says Richard, 'I've often thought there was unused capacity there.'

I drink the gin slowly, making it last. Richard buys us more drinks, salted peanuts, crisps, two pickled eggs on a plate.

'Do you want another of those?'

'I won't be able to stand up.'

'You can lie down. If we go on the beach, right under the prom, no one'll notice us. They'll all be staring out to sea.'

'You're mad, the beach is packed with French students on exchange. You don't think they're interested in the sea, do you?'

'I could buy a towel and we could lie under it. A big one.'

'Yeah, that'd look good.' I think of the white towel humping and twitching like a pantomime horse. Nothing's going to happen, not now. But later, when it's dark, when the food's all eaten and the candles are out. When the table's all wax and scraps and wilted flowers. Then we'll go into the garden, after the party's over.

'I meant it when I said she doesn't sleep with me, you know.'

'I've told you, you don't need to say things like that.'

'I kept trying to get her to tell me the truth about why. Wouldn't you think I'd be old enough to have the sense not to do that? In the end I wore her down and she said she'd married me because she knew I was different from all the other men she'd had. She wanted to break the pattern. But it didn't work, because the men she finds attractive are the sort who aren't any good to her. The men she wants to sleep with. I said that couldn't be true, because the sex was so good for us the first three years. Then she said she'd never felt that way, she'd wanted to but she hadn't been able. Maybe she'd pretended to make me happy. She said she loved me.'

'Why are you telling me all this?'

'I want you to know.'

'Because you still love her and you still wish she'd –'

'No. That's all over.'

He grips my hand hard, his fingers round my knuckles.

'She's right, you know,' I say, 'the men she had never were any good. Not really. She'd get rid of one and then find another just the same.'

'Lots of people do that.'

'And then she met you and she still couldn't make her mind up.'

'You're right there. She was off and on like an undertaker's hat,' says Richard. The pub door bangs open and a woman with bright hair in a tight red dress squints into the dark. The old man in the far corner looks up from his newspaper, sees her, puts the paper on the table and slowly, deliberately, stands. She clicks over to him on her high strappy sandals, shuts her eyes and opens her mouth. They kiss, his hand squeezing her backside.

'I love Brighton,' I say.

'Do you?'

'It's fantastic. You feel you could do exactly what you wanted and no one'd care. Anything could happen. Even the sea looks like a landlord who's going to repossess the place any minute. Look at it parked there at the end of the street, waiting.'

'I didn't notice.'

'Because you've got your bloody eyes shut half the time,' I say, more angrily than I mean to.

'I did notice the colour of the beach-hut doors, though, last time I was here,' he says, picking up my hand, soothing it between his. 'They don't make that blue anywhere else, do they? We'll get a beach-hut, Nina. I'll find out what they cost. You can come down from London and we'll make tea and shut the door and fuck, and then I can nip out and buy you an ice-cream. You'll like that.'

'Listen, we've been here nearly an hour, and we've still got to do the shopping.'

'Let's forget the food. Let's forget the whole thing.' He's leaning against me, his skin hot under the thin white shirt. 'We could do it if you want. We don't have to go back.'

We don't have to go back. We can book into a hotel, not an expensive one on the front but one of the cheaper ones on a street away from the sea. My credit card wouldn't run out for weeks if we took it easy. Let alone the cards Richard must have packing his wallet, along with his doctorates and diplomas. We'd have the full breakfast and picnics on the pebbles. I'd buy a swimsuit. In the evening we'd walk from one Italian restaurant to the next until we found the one we liked. We'd watch the pier lights come on, blotching the night with fantasy. I'd put money on the ten-pence horse-race machine, and we'd buy four fresh doughnuts for a pound and eat them all. When we looked down there'd be water far below between the pier boards, thick and salt and green. And the slime on the metal, the tall, terrifying stanchions. We'd hold hands. Every day we'd see the long-distance swimming club breast-stroke its way past the end of the pier. We'd sit in the Pavilion Gardens at noon watching Japanese tourists eat British sandwiches. One day we'd take a day trip to Dieppe and throw stones out from the beach, back towards ourselves, before we came home clanking with bottles of wine.

We'd stay in, day after blazing hot day. We'd lie skin to skin on the unmade bed while the sun travelled from one side of the dirty window to the other. In the end when our bladders got too full, we'd go down to the little bathroom on the landing, with the notice asking us please to leave these conveniences in the state in which we would wish to find them. There'd be one long hair on the edge of the bath, and a smell of Harpic. Richard would whistle while he shaved and his whistling would coil up the stairs until it reached me. I'd lie there waiting in the state in which he'd wish to find me. One more gin and it'll happen. I lean back and his hand strokes my stomach under the table. He finds my navel and a sharp electric pain goes through to my backbone. Why don't we do it? Phone now and begin to break those threads, one by one.

We won't do it. There's Isabel, Isabel, Isabel. She has spread everywhere and I can't root her out. *I've never blamed you, Neen. I've never blamed you for anything. I love you.* The buttons set deep in the mock leather bench opposite are as black as dahlias. 'We'll have to get the food,' I say.

'Yes, I suppose so.' He yawns and stretches, abandoning

himself to the yawn with a shudder. 'God, I can feel that thunder in my head.'

But when we go out it's as hot as ever, and almost as bright. One small brass-rimmed cloud hangs very high overhead.

Chapter Twenty-four

There's a neat note taped to the top of the windscreen. A little envelope with *'Richard and Nina'* written on it. I unfold it. Inside it says, 'Waited from 1.15 until 2.05. Have gone to get train to Lewes and then taxi. I'll see you both back at the house.' Where did he get the envelope from? Does he carry them round with him all the time? But Richard's ripping open another, official envelope. A parking ticket. On the right side of the windscreen there's a bright yellow sticker which reads *'Authorized for removal.'* Just then, at the top of the street, we see the tow-away truck beginning to back down towards us.

'Get in the car.'

We throw our four carrier bags on to the back seat and jump in. The truck clunks and judders, finding its way through rows of parked cars. 'They make a fucking fortune round here. Just don't try to block me, you bugger. Just don't try.' Richard pulls the wheel round and reverses fast out of the space. 'I bet that bastard Edward phoned them,' he says as we drive away. 'What's he say in the note?'

'Get stuffed. This is going to cost you.'

Richard laughs. 'Good on him.'

'No, he's gone home on the train.'

'We'll be back before him. We could pick him up from the station.'

'Or we could leave him to wait a very long time at the station and then have to pay for a taxi and maybe walk all the way up the track with his shopping.'

'Sounds all right to me. Listen, there's a place up here we can stop for the champagne. Are you sure we got everything else?'

'Yeah, we got everything.'

'I'm not looking forward to this meal.'

'It'll be fine. I wouldn't let you make anything that wasn't.'

'I don't mean the food.'

We're heading up for the bypass, with all the windows rolled right down so hot air thrashes round the car and we have to shout to hear each other. Suddenly Richard pulls in. I've noticed before how he drives as if the passenger knows what he's thinking.

'I won't be a minute.'

I watch him disappear into the wine shop. Behind, you can still see the sea. A faint glitter, like swarf. But the avenues are big and quiet, stunned by heat. It's stiflingly hot now, worse than ever, and the shadows of the trees are blurred. The sky isn't blue any more, but yellow. Richard's right, there's a storm coming, though it might take days to come. The leaves are lustreless and brown with drought, hanging on for rain.

Richard comes out of the shop, balancing the box on his knee as he turns to shut the door. But the shopman comes out after him, in deference to the amount of money Richard's spent. He ushers the box into the boot of the car, says *sir* and *goodbye* and then adjusts the chain on a plastic guide-dog for the blind while he watches us drive off. Richard drops a Mars Bar into my lap. It's cold, solid.

'That's instead of lunch. He kept them in the fridge so it should be all right.'

'I'm sorry, Richard, not on top of the gin.'

The gin's not a dazzle any more, but a sharp, nauseous pain in my stomach. I should have eaten. Pickled eggs and crisps and booze fight one another. The road leaps and twists in front of us. Surely he didn't drive this fast when we were coming the other way. The houses have gone, and now there are white fields, dusty hedges, a man cycling slowly on the cycle track alongside the road.

'Richard, can you stop?'

He glances at me. 'There's a turn-off in half a mile.'

'OK.'

When we stop the silence and stillness rush over me, swamping me. I struggle out of the car and on to the dry grass at the roadside. I kneel down by a patch of nettles and retch but nothing comes up. The thing is to keep still and breathe deeply through my nose. I'm not going to be sick. I put my head down, breathing steadily.

'Here,' says Richard, 'wipe your face with this.'

It's a baby wipe. We bought them in the supermarket along with all the other stuff. It's cool and moist and it smells innocently of baby lotion. I wipe the sweat from my face and neck, and sit back. Fifty yards from us the road hums, but we're quite hidden.

'Are you all right?'

'I'm fine. It was too much gin, that's all.'

'And the excitement,' he says, 'don't forget the excitement.'

'There wasn't enough of that.' Through a gap in the hedge I see a small, framed oblong of landscape. Two fields, a house, a hedge. Perfect and complete, the way other people's lives look.

'What are you looking at?'

'That house through there.'

'Would you like a house like that?'

'I was thinking about how I'd draw it.'

'You haven't got your sketchbook with you, have you?'

'Yes, it's in my bag.'

'Can I look at it?'

'If you want to. I'm not going to draw now, my head's banging.'

He opens the sketchbook, turns a few pages. The cabbage, the cherry-tree bark, a duckling in the huge wake of its mother. Cabbage again. I see him stiffen and then I know what pages he's reached.

'I didn't know you were doing all these.'

He flicks the pages. Ten, fifteen, twenty. I'm surprised myself, because in doing the drawings I didn't realize how many there were.

'Are they all of him?'

'Of Antony, you mean? No, not all.'

There is Antony in Susan's arms. Antony kicking on a blanket in the garden. Antony doubled up with colic, his face creased with anger and anguish. I've drawn him in his bath, with Susan's fingers under his neck supporting his shoulders, and his legs hanging limp as if astonished by the warm water. It must feel so much like home. There he is fastened on to his bottle, all his existence flowing towards the nipple. And in one drawing he sleeps his damp, feathery, solid sleep.

'Has Isabel seen these?'

'No.'

He keeps on turning pages. He stops again, looks closely at these new drawings, and then flicks back a few pages to compare. Then he looks at me.

'These aren't the same. You've made him bigger, haven't you? Look at his legs. And Antony hasn't got that much hair.'

'These drawings aren't of Antony.'

'But surely — they must be. It's the same baby. Look at the shape of the eyes. And the hands, the hands are exactly the same.'

'It's a bigger baby, you were right. This baby's older than Antony. He's three months old. Don't you know who he is? Can't you guess?'

'What do you mean? Am I supposed to recognize him?'

'You've never seen him.'

'Nina, for God's sake, what is this? It's a baby, that's all. Just a baby. It looks like Antony to me but you say it's not.'

'He's Antony's uncle.'

He can't be faking that look of surprise.

'Steve, you mean? Did you do it from a photo?'

I'd forgotten that Richard's got a brother too. 'No, not your brother. Mine. Mine and Isabel's.'

A long breath. 'Oh. I see what you mean.'

'You knew about him, didn't you?'

'I'd forgotten. Isabel did say you had a brother. He died though, didn't he?'

'Yes.'

'So you've done these from a photo of him. How amazing. He looks exactly like Antony.'

'I didn't do them from a photo, I did them from memory.'

'But you must have been tiny. Isabel was only – what? – about eight?'

'Seven.'

'Then you were only four.'

'That's the kind of memory I have.'

Richard turns the pages again, slowly this time. 'I hadn't noticed. He's wearing different clothes from Antony. Different kind of clothes.'

'He wore our baby dresses. My mother put blue ribbons in them. She didn't have enough money to buy new things.'

'I can see the ribbons. You've drawn the ribbons.'

He pores over the book. 'It's extraordinary, Nina. Did you really remember all that?'

'Yes.'

'I never knew you were doing any of these drawings. Isabel will love them. We must have them framed.'

'They're only sketches.'

'Are you feeling better now?'

'Yes, I'm fine. We'd better get on.'

Richard stands up and scans the landscape. 'You can see for miles from here. I was right, look at those clouds beginning to bunch. We're going to get a hell of a storm.'

'It won't come yet.'

'It'll come before tonight,' he says with satisfaction, 'so maybe

I won't have to cook after all. We can drink champagne and watch the lightning.'

'Come on.' I'm shivering a bit, though it's so hot. Nausea makes you cold. I feel as if I can't quite get my breath, as if the air is thick, not air at all. 'Richard, we ought to hurry.'

'It's OK. Edward won't even be off the train yet. We'll still be back before him.'

'We've been away ages. It's all taken much longer than it should have done.'

'Well, we know why that was.'

He's still smiling. He doesn't hurry, though I snatch at the door-handle and yank the seat-belt so hard it jams. He's still in the sunlit foreground of the landscape, in those last moments before the storm hits. Behind him the sky is livid. A small crack of lightning flickers above a tree, and in another part of the picture it's already raining hard.

Chapter Twenty-five

We come in through the garden. It looks as if Susan's just finished the table and gone inside through the open French windows. The heavy linen cloth hangs in glassy folds, and Susan has filled four vases with the black dahlias and white Japanese anemones and placed them down the centre of the table. She's plaited ivy and twined it round the candlesticks. By each plate there's a tiny vase of rosemary or lavender. Everything is carefully, rigidly spaced. But in the centre of the table, between the candlesticks, there's a big fruit bowl I haven't seen before. It's a deep, pure splash of yellow.

'We'll put the figs in that. I'll roll some newspaper balls for them to lie on so they fill the whole bowl.'

We hear footsteps on the wooden boards, and Susan comes out, her arms full of sunflowers.

'Oh, there you are.' She beams at us as if she's our daughter. 'Doesn't it look nice?' Her face is flushed with heat and satisfaction.

'It's beautiful.'

Susan drops half the sunflowers on a garden chair, and their golden faces twist as they settle, looking out through the slats for the sun. 'I'll do these in a minute. Did you get all the food? Where's Edward?'

'He's coming back by train, so he should be here soon. We've got all the stuff in the car.'

'We'd better start bringing it in.'

The garden is perfectly still. What we say seems to have no more meaning than the tap of birds' beaks. What is all this for? The table, the food, the round staring hearts of the sunflowers? What are we playing at here? There's nothing to celebrate.

'Is Isabel still asleep?'

'Oh no,' says Susan, 'she couldn't sleep, so she's gone out.'

'What do you mean?'

Susan pushes her hair back behind her ears. 'Well, she came down and said she couldn't sleep, and I hadn't really got started on anything because of the baby. He took ages to settle after his feed. So Isabel said she'd take him out for a few hours so we could all get on with the meal.'

Richard responds lightly at first, as if to a joke. 'She's taken him out? She can't have. She's not well enough to walk anywhere.'

'She's not going to be walking. She rang for a taxi from the garage. He was going to drive her down to the Gap. It'll be cooler by the water, and then the baby's never seen the sea. It's only five miles.'

Susan must notice the way we're looking at her, but she patters on, 'She said she was going to keep the taxi for the afternoon so he could drive her back as well. She's taken the changing-bag and bottles and everything. I packed it all up for her, I put in three bottles.'

Richard and I look at each other. 'You could have gone with her, Susan.'

'Well, I couldn't really, could I? I mean, there was all this to do.'

There's no blaming Susan. She stands there, pink and upright, clutching flowers. She's done her best, what more can we expect?

'When did she go?'

'It was a bit after twelve. I've got all this done since then.'

She can't resist another quick glance over the table, can't help wishing we'd notice it again. I mustn't give way to the feeling that this thick air isn't really breathable. I clench and unclench my hands to calm myself, and my heart sucks at my ribs. But I always feel like this before a storm, because atmospheric pressure comes into my head like fear. There's nothing to be afraid of now. Isabel's gone out for a change of scene, that's all, for some fresh air by the sea. But even as I click the clichés round in my head they stop working. She'll be on her way back in half an hour, with Antony still asleep in his baby seat. He won't know he's gone anywhere. She'll be smiling her faint smile, remote, surprised that anyone's been worried about her for a moment. Why do I always make such a drama out of everything?

Isabel hasn't been out for weeks, not even in the garden. And then this meal, out of nowhere. A plan, a party. She threw the scent to us and we went chasing off after it. *You and Richard and Nina go and do the shopping. You'll have to go into Brighton to get everything.* Then as soon as we were out of the house she went off in a taxi to the beach, five miles, farther than she's been for months. Because she wanted a change of air. Susan's looking at me.

'What do you think?' Richard asks me, as if Susan's not here.

'I don't know. She ought to be back soon, if she's just gone down to the Gap. And she won't want to get caught in a storm with the baby.'

'No.'

I can't take my eyes off the sunflowers. Where has Susan got so many, and why has she picked them all when they look so much better standing? Their shaggy goldenness spills over the edge of the chair. What will Susan put them in? They're too big for any of the vases. Richard is waiting. Does he think I'm going to know what to do? Susan eyes us both.

'I'd better go and get some water for these sunflowers,' she says, separating herself from us.

'Wait.'

The tension builds. The flowery, festive table jeers: *What party? Did you think there was going to be a party?*

'I think we'd better get down there,' I say.

'And meet her, you mean. Yes, that's a good idea. She won't realize how tiring it is, the first time out.' How responsible we sound. How adult. Then suddenly it hits me like a wave that the house is empty. If I walked round it all, opening every door, I wouldn't find my sister.

'Oh well then,' says Susan, relief in her voice, 'if you're going to do that I'll start getting the plates and glasses out in the kitchen. Mum's bringing the ice-cream over with her. I said eight, was that OK?' She waits, fractionally, but no one answers. 'I bet you meet them coming back. She's gone in Mickey Nye's taxi, from the garage. He's got that red Sierra.' She smiles. You could draw a neat waterproof line right round Susan. We are the ones who are going to sort everything out, and she's Susan, doing her job as well as ever.

'When Edward comes back, tell him we've gone down to meet Isabel,' I say. She nods, already turning and walking crisply into the house.

'I'm sure it's all right,' says Richard as we get into the car. 'But I don't feel too happy about Isabel on her own down there. She's not up to it.' I glance at him while we jab in the ends of our seat-belts, but say nothing.

I went on a self-defence course once, after a man had his throat cut in my street. *Most people get into trouble because they override their instincts,* said the instructor. *Afterwards they'll tell you they didn't like being in the same room with a particular person. They had a bad feeling about him, but they pushed the feeling down because he was a friend, or the gasman or whatever. You've got to learn to listen. Your body'll tell you all sorts of things if you let it. If you get the feeling you want to move away from someone, do it. Move away fast.*

My body is sick with fear. It's so strong I feel it coming out of my pores like sweat. Richard puts the key in the ignition slowly, fiddles with the wing-mirror and then starts the car, and we're halfway down the drive before I remember the food in the back. But I say nothing and hope he won't hear the plastic bags rustle. The food will be spoiling already in this heat, but we can't go back now. At the end of the track Richard turns left, instead of right.

'You're going the wrong way.'

'I know, I'm just going to go up to the garage.'

'She won't be there. He'd bring her straight back to the house. Listen, this is going to take another ten minutes, you're wasting time.'

'Nina, for Christ's sake relax. I can have a word with Janice and find out if Mickey told her what time he was coming back.'

We swing off the road and bump into the dusty courtyard, but even before we stop we've both seen it. A bright red Sierra parked over on the tarmac by the carwash. Richard jumps out of the car ahead of me, and goes across to Janice in the paybooth. 'Janice, is Mickey about?'

She has a pinched face with a ragged pixie haircut round it, and she looks like a child pretending to keep shop. 'He'll be round the back, there's an Espace we've got in for a service.'

Mickey Nye's got the car jacked up and he's rolling away one of the tyres.

'How're you doing, Mr Carrington?'

'Fine thanks, Mickey. Just wondering what time you dropped my wife off down at the Gap.'

'Oh now, it'd be a few hours ago. About half-twelve, it must have been. She said you'd be going down to pick her up later.'

'That's right, we're on our way. This is Isabel's sister, Nina Close.'

'Pleased to meet you.' He grins at Richard. 'Just as well you told me, I'd never have guessed it. You're not much alike for sisters, are you?'

'Did you leave her on the beach?'

'Just by the café. They do a nice cream tea there, and she wouldn't want to be walking far without a pushchair. Still, it's kept fine for her, though they say we're due for a change tonight, and it might come sooner by the looks of it.'

'Yeah, you're right, I want to get Isabel back before it does.'

Our car rocks back on to the road, its tyres spurting dust and stones. I turn and see Mickey Nye staring after us, his wrench in his hand, like a witness saving up what he's seen. 'Why did she say I'd be picking her up?' says Richard.

'It costs a lot to keep a taxi all afternoon. Maybe she didn't know how much till she asked him the price.'

'She told him I was coming. We might have waited all afternoon for her back at the house.'

'She'd have rung.'

Of course she'd have rung. I'm so sure of it I can almost hear the phone ring through the noise of the engine, ringing and ringing in an empty house. I can see Isabel in the old red phone box at the Gap, her back pushed against the door to let in some air, her hair spilling over the receiver. She strains to hear through the noise of kids at the ice-cream van that's always parked near the phone box. The ringing tone goes on and on. She puts down the receiver, stares ahead for a moment, dials again. Six, seven, eight double rings. Susan's down the garden picking more flowers, and we're here, flying down the thunder-dark lane, getting to Isabel as fast as we can. I can't see Isabel's face. Only her hand, clutching the receiver, and her foot rocking the baby in his car-seat so he doesn't wake and start to scream.

It's only five miles. Midges slap against the windscreen, leaving bobbles of blood. Richard turns on the radio and cello music belches from the speakers, yawning and yearning, as we slam down the narrow lanes. And then as we whack round a bend there's a tractor coming towards us, trundling on the crown of the road. The driver's got his ear-muffs on. He keeps coming, waving to us to go back.

'Was there a gate, Nina? Somewhere he can pass?'

'I don't know.'

We reverse, our tyres biting the earth at the side of the lane, but there still isn't enough room. We go back, and back.

'Jesus, if he can't get past here. I'm in the fucking hedge as it is.'

The tractor comes on with dreamlike slowness. It's a boy driving it, a red-faced boy with gum in his mouth. He won't make way for us.

'He's got a football pitch on his left, the stupid bugger.'

The tractor takes our wing-mirror, bends it forward as far as it'll go and snaps it back, shivering the glass into pieces. Through the back window I see the boy's ear-muffed head wagging from side to side to the beat in his headphones, and then our car jumps forward.

There isn't much at the Gap. A café with a pitch-and-putt beside it, some swings and four sagging umbrellas over plastic tables. The beach is made of hard white pebbles and the sea is grey, flat as a table. The light hurts my eyes.

We park the car beside the café, and cross the road to the beach. The hot smell of chip grease follows us. There's the ice-cream van, and the phone box beside it, empty. Visitors sit on mats on the pebbles, in small, muted huddles. They look as if they're waiting for something that hasn't begun yet. There are children in the sea, pushing surfboards around on the flat water. It's one of those lifeless seaside scenes I've seen a thousand times. The day expanded to its fullest point hours ago and now it's seeping away towards evening. It's calm, eerily calm. Where is she? I run a few yards on the pebbles, my feet scrunching and sliding.

'You go the other way. I'll go down to the water.' Richard comes after me. 'No, Nina, she won't have gone down here. Not with the baby.'

But the bubble of panic in my throat is getting bigger and bigger and I flounder on through the heavy shingle until I reach the edge of the breakwater and look down the eight-foot drop. Green, furry weed clings to the black wood, and the tides have heaped up pebbles into great scallops. I'm staring straight down on to the breasts of a topless sunbather who is stretched out with her back arched over a curve of pebble and her eyes closed. Her nipples look back at me, dark and tough.

'Everyone's packing up,' says Richard. 'Let's try the café.'

People are looking up at the sky as they roll towels and mats into bags. Near us a family pulls down its windbreak home. I think I'm going to see Isabel there with them, lying with her face up to the sky. A baby cries and I turn but it's not Antony. There are babies everywhere, in pushchairs and backpacks, or staggering on the pebbles with ice-creams in their hands.

'If we walk right down to the end of the beach and then back . . .'

It doesn't take long. All the holiday-makers are gathered into a strip a few hundred yards wide, and beyond that there are red flags and yellow poles and warnings. I remember Isabel telling me it wasn't safe to swim outside the flags. The water looks calm, but there are currents underneath, and rocks. People don't believe it because it looks as safe as a bath-tub. There are just a few old people walking. How far could Isabel walk, carrying Antony? Surely she won't have come this far. I keep seeing Isabel. The roundness of her head bobbing far out on the water. Isabel is beautiful when she comes up after a dive, her hair streaming and her lashes stuck down, clotted with water. But how could she swim with the baby? Or there, that figure of a woman disappearing into the café, back the way we've come. I'm almost sure she had something in her arms. But she's wearing a blue dress and she doesn't walk like Isabel. The air tears and prickles. 'Thunder,' says Richard, 'did you hear it?'

People are moving faster now, picking up chairs and children, straggling towards the car park. There's a sudden shiver of wind over the sea, breaking the flat surface into oily little waves. Mothers pick their way over the pebbles at the edge of the water and call their children in.

'Lauren! *Rebecca!* I'm not going to call you again.'

But they do. I strain to catch the names, as if one might be the one I want.

'Paul! *Pa -ul!*'

There are names flying everywhere. 'Did you hear that?'

'What?'

'Listen.'

We stand still and another shiver of wind blows Richard's shirt against his body, and then lets it falls loose. 'What did you hear?'

'I thought I heard someone call Isabel. Listen.'

'It can't have been.'

He's right, it can't have been. Isabel wouldn't call her own name like that, as if she was calling herself in from a long way out, so far out that her voice was just a thread in the wind.

Isabel's a good swimmer. We always swam far out, both of us, farther than was safe. We always knew we were safe together. We'd practised life-saving over and over, towing one another in. I would hang in the water with my eyes shut tight while Isabel kicked like a frog and brought me back to the sand. 'You've got to struggle, Neen,' she'd say, but I never did. When we were older we'd talk and talk, out there where no one else could hear, treading water, our voices intimate between the chuckling of the waves. The sea held us up, and we knew we couldn't have sunk if we'd wanted to.

All the mothers are calling their children in now. They want them close by their sides, bare brown legs twinkling to keep up. There are slaps and cries when kids won't come, and then they look up at the sky and they want to come, as fast as they can. One or two big drops of rain fall as we hurry back along the beach.

'She's not here.'

'She must be. She can't have gone anywhere else. She'll have gone inside somewhere.'

'There's only the café.'

'That's where she'll be.'

The drops thicken and spit on the car-park tarmac, and the acrid smell of rain after drought bounces back to us. Far off over the sea, the thunder clears its throat. It's coming fast now. A gust of wind picks up crisp bags and chip wrappers and bowls them over and over.

That's when I look back at the sea one last time. The wind's chopping at it, blowing up foam as it blows in the last few people from the beach. There's the woman who was sunbathing under the breakwater. She has a red T-shirt pulled on over her breasts now, and her hair flaps wildly. She's hurrying to shelter, but then she sees something behind us and she slows to watch it. I turn. That's when I see the police-car sliding down the hill towards the beach. It goes silently and not too fast and there's no siren or flashing light.

Richard has seen it too. 'There can't be anything wrong or it wouldn't be going so slowly,' he says. But we begin to run.

Chapter Twenty-six

Big drops splash us as we run. Everyone's running, across the car park into their cars, or into the covered bus stop. We reach the café door, but we hang back in the shelter of the awning. Richard grasps my wrist. 'You wait here, Nina. I'll go in first.' But I won't let him. Whatever there is to know, I've got to know it too. I look at the grey in his hair and his rain-streaked face and his body in its rumpled summer clothes that look wrong now, with rain whipping down and the light as purple as three-day-old bruising. I want to hide myself in him, to hide him in me. We are so close I hear the catch of breath as he starts to say something, and then decides not to.

'What do you think's happened?' I ask him. 'Where is she?'

'I'm going to report her missing,' Richard answers, and he reaches out and lifts a wet strand of hair away from my mouth. His hands are cold.

'There,' he says, like a mother. He digs in his pocket and pulls out a big cotton handkerchief, and wipes my face with it. 'That's better. Are you all right to go in now?'

The police-car has parked behind us, in the car park. We hear the double clunk of its doors, and then two pairs of feet, almost in rhythm but not quite. They don't run through the rain like everyone else. They walk with their heads down, and the police-woman puts up one hand as a gust of wind tugs at her hat.

Richard pushes open the door and we go in. There's a woman in the café, sitting with her back to us. She's wearing a blue dress, and she has a little boy with her, perched on a chair which is too big for him. He turns to look as we open the café door and his face is pinched and solemn. The woman has a baby in her arms, wrapped in a yellow shawl. I look at the shawl, which I bought in Forever Baby two months before Antony was born. It's a soft yellow, like egg-yolk, and I liked it better than the pastels of the other shawls on display.

'Whatever you do don't get anything pink or blue, Nina. I don't mind yellow.'

Another woman in a flowery pinafore bends over the back of the chair, talking to the woman with the baby. She puts a white cup of tea down on the table in front of her, as if this is a hospital. The café door opens again, and there behind us, like a bad dream in their dark uniforms, are the police. The police-woman has too much make-up on. Her tan looks yellow in this light. The thunder crackles, and a squall of rain hits the window.

'That woman,' I whisper to Richard. 'Look at the baby she's holding.'

The woman with the baby is the important one. The police are with her now, the policewoman crouching down so that her eyes are level with the baby's. She pulls back a corner of the shawl to see his face. All at once the scene is bleached, stopped as if a huge flashlight has gone off. All the faces are rimmed with light as if God has pointed a finger at us.

But it's lightning, only lightning. The air hums with waiting. I count as I always count, and then the thunder slams. It is three miles off, coming closer fast. Richard hasn't seen what I've seen. He's looking at the policeman, not the baby.

I push my way through the people and get to the table, beside the woman, looking down at the baby. The policewoman frowns at me. I put out my hand and pull the fold of shawl right back from Antony's face. He is deep, deep, asleep. I put out my finger and touch his warm forehead. The blood beats in his fontanelle. The policewoman is saying something, but I don't listen. 'The baby,' I ask. 'Where did you get the baby?'

I look from one to another, at the baby, the woman, the baby again. I can't see what these things mean. There is the yellow shawl with its satin fringe, the shawl I bought and posted to

Isabel. This woman must have stolen it with the baby, and that's why the policewoman is here, to search her. There are women like this who steal babies in seaside places, when the mothers are relaxed, sunbathing with their eyes shut.

'She's taken my sister's baby,' I say out loud. Richard touches the policeman's arm and the circle opens like a mouth and takes us in. Faces fall back from us as Richard talks and the policeman listens, writing things down. I lift Antony out of the woman's arms. There's a patch of damp on his shawl.

'He needs changing,' I say.

'I didn't want to wake him,' says the woman. The café owner lifts the counter flap and we all file through. There's a door marked Private and a little room on the other side. Richard and I go first with the baby, then the police and the woman with her little boy.

'Where's Isabel? Where's my wife?' asks Richard.

'We don't know quite what's happened yet, sir,' says the police-woman. 'Can you confirm that this is your baby?'

Richard looks down. He touches the satin edge of the shawl, then the baby's sleeping cheek. 'Yes,' he says. 'Tell me what's happened.'

'We don't know.'

We're in a small room with overalls hanging on the wall. There's a white plastic table, and a chair with a wonky leg. I sit down on the chair. 'I'll get you some tea,' says the café owner.

The baby looks as if he belongs in my arms. 'Right,' says the policeman, and he brings out his notebook, 'so this is your baby, sir. But your wife's not with you. And this is . . .?'

'Of course my wife's not with me. That's why we're looking for her. This is my sister-in-law, my wife's sister.' It sounds so respectable.

'We have to ask,' says the policewoman. 'She might have gone home. Women get funny when they've just had a baby. Forget-ful. We had a woman left her baby behind in the supermarket. It turned out she'd driven all the way home before she remem-bered she'd got a baby.'

'My sister's not like that,' I say.

'You wouldn't believe the things that happen,' says the policewoman.

I never stare at accidents. If I'm travelling somewhere and an ambulance pulls on to the station concourse and two men with a stretcher run towards a train, I don't look. My mother taught me that. You don't watch people when they're being hauled out of one life into another. My mother saw how greedy we were, me and Isabel, how curious, because we thought nothing had happened to us yet. But I'm twenty-nine now and Isabel's thirty-two, and it's a long time since we broke through the wall of backs that hide circles of chaos and sorrow. No one else comes into the little room behind the café. Everyone is standing, except me, and then the café owner brings in more plastic chairs and they clash against each other as everyone else sits round the table. There's no window, so we can't see the storm, but we hear the thunder overhead, and the drive of rain on the roof. For long periods, I forget the storm altogether as the woman who was holding Antony talks to us and to the police.

Chapter Twenty-seven

What began then, in the back-room of the café, is still going on. Bits of the story fit together one way, and then another. From time to time a new piece is brought in and we have to move everything around.

At around 1.30 p.m. Isabel spread out her green striped towel over her new beach mat and sat down on the beach within a few yards of Mrs Patricia Newsome, who was spending the day at the Gap with her son Lewis, aged four. There was plenty of space on the beach and Pat Newsome remembers thinking that she'd chosen to sit rather close, and that perhaps it was because of being alone with what was obviously a very new baby. Before that Isabel had paid off Mickey Nye outside the Oasis Café, had bought a tube of Factor 25 sun-cream and a Japanese beach mat, and crossed the road to the beach. The driver of a Volkswagen Estate remembers braking because she seemed to be having difficulty in crossing the road, with the baby seat in one hand, the changing bag, beach mat and handbag in the other. She walked very slowly.

The baby started to cry and Isabel gave him his bottle. While she was doing this she got talking to Pat. They exchanged first names.

'I'm Pat, and this is Lewis. Say hello to the lady, Lewis. He's a bit shy.'

'Hello, Lewis, I'm Nina.'

Pat is quite clear on this point. She remembers mentally adding Nina to her list of possible names for a girl: Pat is six months pregnant with her second child, and she wants a girl. She thought Nina might be nice for a second name. I know almost every word Pat and Isabel said during the afternoon: at least, I think I do. Sometimes it occurs to me that Pat is keeping back or has forgotten something which might sound just like any other detail, but will be the key to everything. But the more I look at Pat's clear, pale, pregnant face the less I can believe that she'd deliberately hide anything.

'I'm Nina,' I say as I sit with the baby in my arms. 'It was Isabel you were talking to.'

'What do you mean?'

'My name's Nina. Hers is Isabel. She gave you my name instead of hers.'

'What would she want to do that for?'

'I don't know. Maybe she was thinking about me.'

'You're close,' says Pat, 'I can tell. This must be terrible for you.' Her grey eyes stare at me and I know that Nina has been crossed off the mental list of names for her child. But Pat can't give me back those hours she shared with Isabel.

'How did she seem when you were talking to her?'

'Oh well, you know, a bit tired. As soon as she sat down I didn't think she looked well, but then she'd just had a baby. She told me it was the first time she'd been out with him. We talked about learning to drive so she could get out more. She was very nice to Lewis.'

When we were little Isabel and I would turn to look at accidents. We wanted to force our way inside that circle of things happening. We thought that nothing important had ever happened to us. Or perhaps I was the only one who thought that, and Isabel knew better.

'It must have been about half-past one,' says Pat. 'No, it'd have been a bit later than that, because we'd had our picnic, hadn't we, Lewis? She was giving the baby his bottle and we got talking. You do, don't you, when you've got children. Lewis couldn't believe how tiny the baby was. He kept asking, could the baby make a sandcastle, could he go swimming. She hadn't brought a flask so she asked me if I'd keep an eye on the baby while she went and got a coffee. She brought a lolly back for Lewis as well.'

The little boy's eyes flick from face to face, uncomprehending. 'Lady give me a lolly,' he says.

'That's right, she was a nice lady, wasn't she? So we got talking. She told me it was the first time she'd taken the baby out. I told her how frightened I'd been of taking Lewis out when I first had him. I was always afraid I'd be stuck somewhere and have to breast-feed him with people looking.'

'I'm not breast-feeding Colin,' she said.

Richard's face doesn't change. He's leaning forward, a bit blank, as if he can't quite hear what she's saying. Perhaps he's forgotten who Colin is again. The policewoman keeps on writing things down. I look at the little boy's face and realize that he has seen Isabel, maybe even touched her. He's part of those hours we're trying to piece together. Isabel smiled at him and said hello. She gave him a lolly, and she sunbathed for a while before it clouded over. She said she ought to change the baby's nappy, but she didn't, although Pat saw she'd brought everything with her. The baby was only wet, not dirty. 'We were just chatting. Nothing special. Just about babies. She was very pale and I asked her if she'd be all right getting home, because I could give her a lift if she wanted. I knew she'd come in a taxi but they're not always easy to get down at the Gap, not in the season. But she said her husband was coming to pick her up.'

My sister was wearing a black swimsuit, and a yellow sarong tied round her waist. She rubbed Factor 25 sun-cream into the baby's face and arms, even though it was quite cloudy by then. Pat noticed that she was extremely careful over everything she did for the baby, and she didn't seem sure she was doing the right things. She was very anxious about him. She asked Pat if she thought she'd put enough cream on.

'He'll be fine if he's got your skin,' said Pat, looking at Isabel's smooth, golden shoulders. But Isabel glanced up from rubbing in cream and said, 'Oh no, he won't look like me.'

Pat thought that was a strange thing. Isabel seemed so sure, as if she'd looked into the baby's future. And you'd think that a woman who looked like Isabel would hope to pass it on to her children, even if she wasn't vain, which Isabel obviously wasn't.

'I can't stand those women who get themselves up like models, everything perfect,' says six-months-pregnant Patricia Newsome. But she liked Isabel.

'Look at him,' said Isabel, and she held out the baby flat on her forearms, as if she was offering him on a tray to Pat. Pat said the baby was gorgeous.

'Do you think so?' Isabel asked. She looked at the baby for a long time, then she put him down to sleep.

At about three o'clock, or a bit later, Isabel stood up suddenly, then picked up the baby. Pat wondered if she'd caught sight of her husband, who was coming down to fetch her. Already Pat felt a bit curious about what the husband of this woman might be like. She says this, and then flushes faintly, looking at Richard. 'Only because she was different,' she says.

'How do you mean, different?' asks the policeman, but Pat only repeats, quietly and surely, 'She was different.'

Isabel said that she was going to go for a walk. She wanted to stretch her legs.

'Don't go too far,' Pat said. She still doesn't know why she said it, except that Isabel looked so pale.

'Oh no, I shan't. I'll just take the baby along the beach and show him the sea, then I'll get something to eat from the café. I'm starving.'

'Are you sure Isabel said that?'

'What?'

'"I'm starving."'

'Oh yes, she said she hadn't had anything to eat since break-fast. I offered her a sandwich but she said she wanted something hot. But she really didn't look well and I didn't think she ought to carry the baby all that way. She'd left the baby with me while she got her coffee, so I thought I'd ask if she wanted me to watch him for her again. He was fast asleep, he'd be no problem. I said to her, "I'll mind the baby if you like. I expect you could do with half an hour's peace and quiet." But she didn't want to. She said, "No, he's got to come with me." I knew how she felt, because I was funny about leaving Lewis with anyone at first, even my mum. And she didn't really know me. So I said, "It'd be lovely for Lewis. I'm trying to get him used to the idea of babies. You'd be doing me a favour, really." Then she said, "Would I? Are you sure?"

"Course I'm sure. You pop him back in his car-seat and we'll both keep our eye on him, won't we, Lewis?"

'She put him in, and did up the safety-straps. Then she put the blanket over his feet, though it wasn't really cold. She knelt down there for a minute, then she said, "Are you sure I shouldn't take him with me?" "I'm not going to run off with him," I said, "I couldn't run far like this, anyway." She smiled and then she got up, took her purse out of the changing-bag and went away up the beach.'

She smiled and got up, then she took her purse out of the changing-bag and went away up the beach.

'Did you watch her?'

'I'm sorry?'

'Did you watch her go away – up the beach?'

'Well, no, I didn't. I had Lewis, you see, and the baby.'

'Of course.'

I'd have watched if I'd been there. Even if Isabel hadn't looked back, I'd have seen her bare feet picking carefully over the stones, her long, fine brown legs, the yellow sarong, her bare back in the scooped black swimsuit.

'When did you start to get worried?'

Pat flushes. 'As soon as she'd gone. I really did, I'm not just saying it. There was something about her. You felt she needed looking after. To tell the truth I was surprised anyone'd thought she was well enough to come out on her own. She didn't look as if she knew what to do.' Pat looks at me and Richard. 'I don't know why I'm saying all this to you. You know her much better than I do.'

'Go on.'

'There was something wrong, wasn't there?'

'Yes, sir, it would help if you could let us have some background,' says the policeman. But just then the café owner comes to the door. A man has come into the café with a woman's purse. It's got a name in it.

He found Isabel's purse farther along the beach, where the red flag flies all the time. It wasn't down near the water nor up by the road, but about halfway between, lying on the shingle. That was when the policeman got up quietly and went out to make some phone calls.

There was nothing missing from Isabel's purse. In it there was £18.42 in cash, a credit card, a cheque card, four receipts in a zip compartment, a scrap of paper with a telephone number on it, and a tiny black-and-white photograph which I hadn't seen for years. The photograph showed a little girl holding a doll. Her eyes squinted against the sun and her fringe was blown back by the wind off the sea. It was me, standing outside our house in St Ives. I must have been about four. *Nina Close, 6 Channel Terrace, St Ives, Cornwall, Great Britain, the World.* The doll was Rosina, not Mandy. Isabel must have let me hold her for the photograph. I am smiling at the camera and my arms are a proud, exaggerated cradle.

A long time later I tried the telephone number Isabel had written on the scrap of paper, but all I got was an electronic voice repeating: *The number you have dialled has not been recognized.*

Chapter Twenty-eight

The sky looks like a junkyard. Searchlights and car headlights and flashing torches crisscross in ugly patterns as they bounce off nothing. My eyes sting from looking at them. It's ten o'clock now and the search for Isabel has been going on for so long that it's grown into me, a new way of life that will never end. People come in with cups of coffee and whispered messages. Tyres churn on the shingle. Most of the time I hold the baby, except when I hear something and I have to find out what's going on. I heard a siren and I went out and an ambulance was bouncing down the road, its big suspended backside rocking slowly. There was a blue light revolving on the top. I started running but the policewoman called me back. It wasn't Isabel, it was one of the searchers who'd fallen from a breakwater. He'd broken a leg but he was all right.

Richard went out in one of the boats, wrapped in oilskins. They didn't want him to go because the conditions were so bad, but he went anyway. I watched the boat slip and rock on the water with the tide running anyhow and the storm still roaring. When Richard came back he was shivering.

'It's so black,' he said, 'You can't see anything.' His eyes were shocked and wide. 'There's so much water,' he said, 'you'd never find anyone out there. And the lights make it worse.' The policewoman brought him some tea, her face saying that he shouldn't have gone. Antony was grizzling and I put my finger in his mouth to keep him quiet, the way I'd seen Susan do. He sucked hard. Three nights ago Isabel was in the bath while I washed out her bras and pants in the wash-basin. 'Look, Neen,' she said, and she squeezed the skin around her breasts until milk came out into the water like thin smoke. We watched the milk roll away through the bath water until it dissolved.

'Have you tasted it?' I asked her.

'Mm.'

'What's it like?'

'Sweet. A bit like Milky Bar. You can try if you want.'

The storm has growled away inland now, beyond the Downs, but it's still raining, a fine, steady rain. The helicopter's back again, trundling low in the air, with its big white beam spreading down to the water. The rotors make a noise like an electric whisk at full power. Things are happening here which belong safely on the news, but we can't switch them off. Richard's just walked down to the edge of the water for the hundredth time. There's his hunched shape, tramping down the pebbles with a big searchlight shadow thrown behind it. I glance down at Antony, asleep in his car-seat. He'll be fine for a few minutes.

I am wet by the time I get to Richard. He's standing on the shingle a few feet above the water's edge. I come up behind him and put my arm through his. He jumps, jerking my arm, sending the jar all through me.

'It's all right, it's me.'

'Did I hurt you? I didn't mean to pull you like that.'

'I should have thought.'

'You were so wet, you see –'

'You thought it might be her.'

'Yes.' His face shines with rain.

'I'm sorry. You were waiting and thinking –'

'I wasn't.' He says it abruptly, with hostility. 'I wasn't waiting for her, if that's what you think.'

I listen to the waves break. The tide's turning. It has that wildness water has at the moment when it changes direction.

You should never bathe on a falling tide. If I stepped into that water now it'd take me to where Isabel's gone. I could find her now.

'She's gone,' Richard says, his voice flat and final. 'She's done what she wanted.'

'They think it was an accident.'

'Of course it wasn't. You know that as well as I do.'

A long tongue of sea rushes in, spilling white over my feet. It's cold. The last big wave before the tide turns. I think with horror that he believes Isabel killed herself because she knew about us.

'It's been coming for years,' says Richard. The hard, dull thumps of my heart are so loud I can hardly speak over them. Heat floods me. 'She's got what she wanted,' he repeats.

'Nobody wants this,' I say.

'If you cut out all the other options, then this is what you're left with.'

'She had the baby. She can't have meant to kill herself. Women with babies don't kill themselves.'

'God knows why she had him,' say Richard. 'But she was always so fucking obstinate. She always had to do what she fucking well wanted. Everyone else could go and fuck themselves.'

He is crying, making that raw belly-noise men like him make when they cry.

'It wasn't your fault,' I shout over the noise of the sea. 'It was nothing to do with you.'

But he goes on crying and the sea grinds the stones as it goes down, and the wind slaps my face.

A different policewoman comes in with a baby bottle in her hand.

'Here you are.' She is proud of herself. I ran out of bottles for

Antony, so she's driven five miles and got a chemist to open up and sell her some baby-milk. I find the money for her and think how strange it is to be buying baby-milk from a policewoman in the middle of the night. 'Is this café always open so late?' I ask.

'Oh yes. It's the only place round here so they do good business. The kids come in, so we usually keep an eye. There was a bit of trouble with drugs a couple of years ago. Joe boiled up your bottle for you, so you don't need to worry, it's sterile.'

She talks as if I am Antony's mother. The milk is just the right temperature, and Antony's moaning in his car-seat, not yet awake but sensing hunger below the threshold of sleep. Or maybe it's the noise of the helicopter that's disturbed him. He's slept for hours. I've never known him sleep as he's slept this evening. The whack of blades gets louder as the helicopter sweeps in over the sea towards the café, and the baby's face twists as he lets out his first cry. I think, 'They're searching for your mother. That's what woke you,' but I can't believe in it. The policewoman goes to the window and looks up as I rub the teat against Antony's lips and then nose it into his mouth. Without opening his eyes, he begins to suck greedily.

'Where are they going now? Are they going to try inland?'

She looks at me, her face guarded. 'I don't think so.' She pauses. 'It looks to me as if they're calling off the search for tonight, but I could find out for you.'

'But they haven't found her.'

'The thing is, once it gets this dark it's like looking for a needle in a haystack, even with the lights.'

'So they aren't going to look any more.'

'I didn't say that. They'll start again at first light, and they'll go on all day if they need to.'

'But it'll be too late. She can't possibly –'

My mind blanks. I think of Isabel out there in the streaming darkness. It's cold after the storm, and in the sea it'll be colder. The waves are chopping up against the beach, and that means it'll be rough farther out. Even a strong swimmer like Isabel would find it hard. 'If she's in the water, things don't look so good,' says the policewoman, 'But then we don't know that she is.'

'What do you mean?'

'People do go off. They get upset. They hide out somewhere. You'd be amazed how often a missing person turns up.'

'But nobody's seen her. Where could she have gone to?'

Maybe she walked farther along the beach than anyone believes she could walk. She might have found a crack in the chalk cliffs where the overhang kept her dry in the storm. She might be there still, huddled on herself, waiting. The policewoman doesn't answer. She's been here for hours and she must be tired too. She's saying the right things by rote while her eyes want to be elsewhere.

'He's enjoying that bottle,' she says.

The way she says it makes me ask, 'Have you got children?'

'One. A little boy, he's two.' She almost smiles at the thought of her child, then straightens her face again. They still think Isabel's had an accident. Or that's what they tell us they think. It was hot and she suddenly decided she'd like to go for a swim. They know that when she left Pat she didn't go to the café. No one saw her again at the café or the shop or in the car park. The buses have been checked, and local taxi firms. Nothing. She might have walked along the beach in that heavy heat just before the storm, and thought that a quick dip would make her feel better. She didn't realize it wasn't safe to swim outside the flags. Isabel, who lived in St Ives until she was eighteen, didn't realize what a red flag meant. There are never many people down that part of the beach, and so it's not too surprising that no one saw her. She went into the water and off the shelf, out of her depth. There's an undertow. She was still weak after the birth, and she could have got into difficulties very quickly. That's their story.

'She was a strong swimmer,' I said. 'Isabel got her gold survival medal when she was ten. We were brought up by the sea.'

I was afraid they'd give up too soon, while Isabel was still swimming, her hair spreading out on the sea around her with each stroke, up then down, her face wet but still above water. The salt water would hold her up. She wouldn't panic, she'd keep swimming. I must hold on to that picture of Isabel swimming, or she'll give up. She'll sink, and try to cry out, and drown.

Richard comes in and sits beside me. His face looks empty now and almost peaceful. It is so quiet we hear the wheeze of air escaping from the bottle as Antony sucks. Then Richard says, 'There's nothing out there, Nina. They say we should go back. They're starting again as soon as it gets light.'

They're stopping. They'll turn out the lights, and the easy black of sea at night will sweep over everything. Maybe the helicopter's already landed. Everyone's going to go home, and tell the story to their wives or husbands, and then have a drink and talk about something else.

'Let's wait a bit,' I say.

'You'll be better off at home,' says the policewoman, 'and we'll contact you the moment we hear anything. You need a hot bath and some dry clothes.' She keeps telling me to call her Elaine but I forget. She says the right words but her voice is tired and she wants to be at home, too, stripping off her concern with her uniform. She's had enough of us. I turn to Richard, 'But we've got to wait, Richard, because Isabel –' I don't want to say this in front of the policewoman, but she sits stolidly on. She's listening. She's been trained to wait a long time for what she wants to hear.

'– Isabel wouldn't come back while there was all this light and noise. You know how she'd hate it. She'd wait until it was dark again. She might have fallen asleep somewhere. You know how tired she was.'

There's a tap at the door and the policewoman gets up. 'I won't be a moment,' she says.

'Nina,' says Richard, 'we've got to get back. Susan and Edward are still waiting.'

'Jesus. I'd forgotten about them.'

'Yes, I know, but they've been waiting for hours. Edward would've come down if I hadn't said he ought to stay at the house in case Isabel phoned.'

The door opens again and the policewoman comes back in, with a different policeman, one we haven't seen before. He nods, and sits down on the other side of the table.

'I'm sorry. I'm afraid we've had a call in response to an item we put out on local radio a couple of hours ago, and it's not good news.' He pauses and the air in the room thickens, as if it's filling up with water. I pick up a cigarette butt from the ash-tray and shred the paper. Tobacco falls out in golden threads. The policeman looks at Richard, and then at me, his big seamed face close to us as he leans forward. I have the strangest feeling that I know this policeman well, that I've slept with him once long ago, but I can't remember it clearly. The atmosphere is charged, sexual, appalling. I want to stop his mouth with my lips.

'A gentleman has phoned in who recognized the description of your wife. He said he saw a woman answering to her description walking down towards the water, in the red flag area. She waded in and although he was just leaving the beach he ran back down to warn her that it wasn't safe to bathe there. He said he thought she looked ill. She told him not to worry, she knew the coast and would be quite safe. She wanted to –' The policeman clears his throat.

'What?' Horror swarms over my skin. What had Isabel said?

'She wanted to get cool. He said something about having had enough of this hot weather, and she said she had too, she'd be glad when it was over.'

'Is that all she said?' Richard asks.

'That's what he told us, sir. Just chit-chat about the weather. But he looked back when he got to the top of the beach, and she was still standing there in the water, looking out to sea. It stuck in his mind. So as soon as he heard the news item, he rang in.'

The oily sea licks round Isabel's thighs. She's the only one in the water. The bulge of shingle and the breakwater hide her from the main beach. The man stands and watches her from the top of the beach. If he put up a finger he could blot her out, but she sticks in his mind. He sees the deep scooped back of her black swimsuit, her yellow sarong hanging limp around her, the cloth dragging and wet. Everything is grey and horizontal and still except Isabel.

'People make these things up,' says Richard harshly, 'trying to get in on the action.'

'I'm sorry, sir. It was definitely your wife he was talking to. He gave us details that weren't in the description we put out. I'm very sorry.'

He sits back, and I know he thinks it's over. When the man went out of sight she would have moved. She would have waded deeper and deeper into the lifeless water. She might have thought how different it was from the purple and turquoise sea we grew up in, or she might have thought of nothing at all. I know there comes a point when you think of nothing at all. Then suddenly the shelf of pebble ended and she walked on water. She walked in and the water went over her head. But it's not so easy to drown, and Isabel knew that. Maybe that's what she was thinking of when she told the man she would be glad when it was over.

Chapter Twenty-nine

Here I am in Isabel's garden. The rain has stopped, but everything is wet, drooping over with the weight of water. There's a smoky smell in the air, like the smell of chrysanthemums. I walk down the path to the cherry tree. A small, misty moon gives enough light for me to see where I'm going. Behind me, every window of the house blazes. Susan turned all the lights on, waiting for us to come back.

Edward's gone. When Richard told him the search had been called off he said, 'I'm going down there.' I thought Richard would try to argue him out of it, but he didn't. He said, 'I'll take you.'

'Don't bother. I'll get a taxi,' said Edward.

'But you must have something to eat first,' Susan said. 'You look terrible.' Margery has been here, making soup. Every sign of Isabel's feast has been cleared away: the table, the cloth, the flowers. There's a black bin-bag slumped by the cooker. I picked it up and it weighed next to nothing. It was full of sunflowers and Japanese anemones and black dahlias. I'd already thrown all the food we bought in Brighton into a council bin down at the Gap. More figs than I'd ever had before, perfect inside their bloomy skins. In the rush we'd chucked them into the back of the car anyhow and they were jammy, discoloured, oozing seed.

Margery is wonderful in a crisis. She was made for wars and sieges, not the Young Farmers. The house throbbed like a general's headquarters, with Margery fielding the telephone. She came in from the kitchen carrying a tray of strong coffee and her gaze swept us all, Edward, Richard, me. 'I'll ring for a taxi,' Edward said, and he disappeared into the hall. I heard him moving about upstairs, and when he came down he had his bag with him. 'The taxi'll be here in quarter of an hour,' he said.

'But what will you do down there? There's nowhere to sit. They've shut the café.'

'I'll wait. It'll be light again in a few hours.'

He wanted to be near Isabel, in the last place where she'd been, and he didn't want us there. 'Richard,' he said, and then stopped.

'What?'

'I want to go in Isabel's room.'

'Isabel's room?'

'Yes.'

'Well, of course, if you want to.' *Why are you asking me?* hung in the air. After all Edward was in the house all evening. He could have been in Isabel's room for hours if he'd wanted.

'The door's locked.'

'It can't be. She never locks her door.'

'I've tried it. And I can't find the key.'

'I didn't even know there was one.'

But there is. It was Susan who found it. She looked up on the lintel and saw an edge of metal. 'There it is!'

It fitted and turned and the door opened. There was the bed she shared with Richard, with the covers pulled smooth and tight. She slept there alone before he came. It's always been Isabel's room. The air smelled of Isabel: her body, her perfume, her clothes. Her nightdress hung loose over a chair. The window was wide open, letting in the cool night air, and there was a patch of damp on the boards where the rain had blown in. Isabel hadn't expected rain, even though she'd been saying every day that the garden needed it. I looked at the stain on the boards. The carelessness of it, the way rain could fall there as if on to an upturned face.

'I'll stay here for a bit, if that's all right,' said Edward, 'until the taxi comes.' He wanted us to go. We backed out of the room and as the door closed I realized that this was probably the last time Edward would ever be in this house, where he's come time after time, spending days and weeks here. Why should he come any more? This house meant Isabel. We shut the door and left Edward standing in the middle of Isabel's room.

He came down ten minutes later, silent, his face stiff. The taxi was waiting at the top of the track with its engine running.

'We'll be down later,' said Richard, and Edward nodded, but still he said nothing. Susan was crying. We all waited in the hall, listening to the taxi turn and then go off down the track, and then Margery came and said she'd made bacon and eggs, and the best thing to do was eat them and go to bed. We'd have a long day tomorrow.

But the long day of today is still going on. My clothes are soaked from brushing against wet leaves. I am by the dahlias now. I run my hands over the bristling stems where Isabel cut off the flowers with her secateurs, and then I walk on. All the scents are coming out in the wet air. I walk past jasmine, and tobacco flowers. Everywhere there's the sharp smell of rain on parched earth, and the garden sucks and rustles around me. I keep thinking I can hear the river, though I know I can't. If I climbed up and stood on the wall I might see the shine of it as it makes for the sea five miles off. I sit down on the seat and listen to drops of water falling off the leaves around me and pocking on the ground.

I must have fallen asleep. At once Isabel is beside me, in her green gingham dress. Her bare legs are thin and scratched, and she has a pair of battered sandals on her feet.

'You've come back,' I say, and my heart floods with relief.

'Don't be silly, Neen, I only went ahead to see if you could manage it. I think you'll be OK. Come on.' She takes my hands and leads me round the bulge of a cliff. We are walking on packed, damp sand, and a wave runs in over our sandals, then another. 'Quick, the tide's coming in,' says Isabel. 'We'll have to hurry.'

We've done it again. We've walked round the headland, forgetting the time as we paddled and jumped from rock to rock. Beyond each rock-pool there's another, and another. We dig with driftwood in coves of white sand, and decorate our castles with shells and red seaweed. Now the tide's coming in and we can't get back in time. We're going to have to climb the cliff. There's nothing to be frightened of because we've often had to do it before, and the cliffs are not as high here as they are farther down the coast. I'm four years old and I climb like a crab. But we've never gone so far before.

'Here,' says Isabel, 'we've got to get up these steps.'

They don't look like steps to me. They're too big. They are high and hard and they go up the cliff in tight zigzags.

'Smugglers' steps,' says Isabel.

'Are they really, Isabel?'

'You can tell by those hooks in the rock. Look. Those are for hauling up the contraband.'

The lowest hook is just above my head. I reach up and touch the rusty iron, then snatch my hand away. A wave washes the back of my legs, nearly to my knees. The steps are slippery at the bottom with seaweed hanging off them like green hair.

'Come on, Neen. You can't wait there. I'll go first.'

'Isabel! I can't get up this step.'

'Of course you can. Here. Put your knee up there, like that, now grab my hand.'

'I don't want to, Isabel. Let's go back the way we came.'

'We can't. The tide's coming in too fast.'

'We could swim. I can swim now, can't I, Isabel?'

'Don't be so stupid, Neen, you can't swim in this. Look at it.'

The tide swirls round my legs, pushing me against the rock. It falls back then pushes me again, harder, almost knocking me over.

'*Quick*, Neen!'

She hauls me up, my knees scraping over the rock. One big step, then the next. 'You have to hold on to the hooks as well. Hold my hand, and hold the hooks. That's right.'

'What if we get stuck?'

'We won't get stuck. I've climbed this cliff millions of times.'

'Have you really, Isabel?'

We keep climbing. Once I slip on a patch of seaweed and bang my head hard on the rock, but Isabel hauls me back upright.

'You've got to hold on tight, Neen!'

I look up at the cliff above us. It goes on for ever, the great slippery steps, the iron hooks which are too big for my hands.

'It's all right, Neen, I've got you. Look, we're nearly at the top. You wait here and hold on to this. I'll climb up then I'll turn round and pull you. Hold on tight.'

The sea moves hungrily below us, like our cat pacing up and down under the nest in the lilac bush in our back yard. I'm always afraid the babies will fall out.

'The sea wants us to fall,' I say quietly, so that it won't hear. Isabel doesn't hear me either. She's climbing. The steps are cut even wider here, for men's legs, not ours. She puts her hands on the edge of the shelf and pushes herself up. Her strong brown legs beat wildly in the air and then she's up, scraping her knees over the lip of the rock. I hold on tight to the hook, with rusty flakes of iron cutting into my palm. Isabel's face appears over the edge of the rock. One of her arms is wound round the next hook, and the other is reaching down for me.

'Come on. I'll help you up this bit.'

She smiles. Her hair blows round her face but she hasn't got a free hand to push it away.

'You climb and I'll pull.'

But I can't let go of the iron hook. I stare up at where Isabel is, then down at the waiting sea. 'Don't look down, Neen! Look at me.' But I hang back. Isabel's face changes. 'If you don't come, Neen, I'm going to go on up and leave you there.'

I stare at her in horror. She kneels up, stands with her back to me and reaches for the next handhold. *'Isabel!'*

'Come on then. Let go of that hook and grab my hand and I'll pull you up. Come on or I'm going without you.'

Sobbing with terror I shut my eyes and lunge for Isabel's waiting hand. The rock tears my legs as she drags me up and I claw my way over the edge with my free hand. I roll against the rock-face and curl up tight, shutting myself up against the sea and Isabel. Isabel kneels beside me. 'It's all right, Neen. The other steps are easy. We're nearly at the top.'

'You said you were going to leave me down there on my own.'

'I had to say that or else you'd never've come. I didn't mean it.'

After a minute I stop crying, uncurl myself and we go on up the cliff, Isabel first, and me following, holding her hand.

I open my eyes. 'Isabel,' I say. The dry plants suck up the rain around me. I've slept and while I was sleeping the water went into Isabel's mouth and she drowned.

'She couldn't have swum for long,' Margery said as we drank our coffee, meaning to console us, 'not after that operation. She was so weak.' She meant that Isabel didn't have time to be afraid. But I know the sea and I know it's not as easy as that. Time at sea is different from time on land. I look at my watch.

It's two o'clock now, and in less than three hours it'll be getting light. Morning will come, bringing Edward's cold face and the police and the rawness of everything. I walk on, feeling my way past branches which dip low with their weight of rain. An apple knocks my cheek and my feet wade in sprawling flowers.

'Nina,' says Richard.

'I thought you'd gone to bed.'

'I couldn't. I knew you'd be out here.'

'I had a dream about Isabel.'

Our cold hands touch, then hold. 'Margery's gone, and Susan's got the baby in with her,' says Richard. 'He's been no trouble tonight, has he? Nina, you're soaking wet.'

'I'm all right.'

His hands touch my shirt, my jeans. 'You're wet through.'

'Yes. Soaked to the skin.'

'You ought to take those clothes off.'

'I know.'

'Nina –'

'It's OK, Richard.'

He drags me to him and we sway, clinging together, my wet clothes against his. 'I've been looking everywhere for you,' he says. 'I thought you'd gone. I've been all over this fucking garden in the dark trying to find you. Round and round these bastard paths that don't go anywhere. It's a nightmare.'

'I was out here all the time.'

'I was afraid you'd gone.'

He shoves his head into my shoulder and I feel his lips sucking my neck, blistering the skin. He'll raise marks. I pull back.

'I want you so much,' he says.

'I know,' I say. I watch his tangled head, his big hot body butting against mine. There is no Isabel any more.

'Where can we go? Let's go, Nina. Let's get out of here.'

'We've got to stay.'

'It's a nightmare,' he repeats. 'I've always hated this fucking garden.' His weight is on me, pushing me down. 'The ground's wet,' I say.

'Nina.' He wraps both arms round me and squeezes me tight, tight.

Death makes people want to fuck. Who said that? Someone at work, after coming back from a funeral. American Paul. *I've never felt so horny. But there was no one there I could screw, so I ate a bowl of potato chips.* I am under Richard, my head scrubbed into the muddy ground. I wriggle and pull down my jeans, then raise my hips. He is hot and I'm cold, freezing, as if I've been out in the rain a long time. I can't stop myself shivering.

'I'll make you warm,' he says. He kneels and kisses the mound of my stomach, sucking and licking. I look up over his shoulder at the sharp black leaves and the mist and the moon. I'm cold and shrunken and it hurts when he comes inside me.

'You weren't ready,' he says afterwards. 'I'm sorry.'

'It's all right.' I pull up my clammy jeans over my bare flesh, zip them and fasten the button. He puts one hand on each side of my face, framing it. His hands are warm and it's a gentle gesture, perhaps the gentlest that's ever passed between us. It almost melts me.

'I'm a selfish bastard. You must be dead on your feet.'

'I'm all right. It's just that everything feels so strange. I think I need to sleep. You'll wake me up, though, won't you? You wouldn't leave me behind? I want to go down there as soon as it's light.'

'I'll wake you.'

'Richard. I want to sleep in Isabel's room.'

He takes in a breath against my cheek. 'Why, Nina? What's all this about Isabel's room? There's nothing there.'

'Were you going to sleep there?'

'No. I'll grab a couple of hours downstairs on the sofa.'

'Then you won't mind if I do.'

'If you want to.'

'Just for tonight.'

Chapter Thirty

Richard stumbles, puts out his hand to the wall and leans there. He gazes stupidly at the table, his eyes black with fatigue. Wave after wave it washes through him. *What she fucking well wanted. Everyone else could go and fuck themselves. If she's in the water. Things don't look so good.* My golden Isabel with the fish prodding her, sly as rats.

'You need some brandy.'

I fetch the bottle from the kitchen cupboard, and two glasses, and take them into the sitting-room, where he's sitting on the sofa, knees apart, head down, hands covering his face.

'You drink this, and then you'll sleep.' I fill his glass to the top with the pale expensive cognac that Richard's always bringing back from trips abroad. When he brought this bottle home in its tacky presentation box inside the plastic airport carrier, Isabel was there. She wrote down in her diary: *R back from X.* He drinks his way steadily down the glass, making a trustful noise like a child drinking milk. His eyes are half-closed.

'Have some more.' I splash it into his glass and drink from my own, but not too much, just enough to warm me. I can't sleep yet.

'Lie down there and I'll get you a blanket. I won't be a minute.'

In the hall there's a blanket box where Isabel keeps bedding for people to sleep downstairs when all the bedrooms are full. I drag out a thick black-and-red blanket, and a pillow. By the time I get back he's lying full-length, his eyes open a slit, and he's sucking in air through his mouth.

'I've got you a pillow. Here, lift your head.'

'That's excellent,' he says in a loud, strange voice, but he's already asleep.

I push the pillow in under him, drape the blanket over the mound of his body, and then tuck it in at his feet and stand back, looking down at him. I'll have to set the alarm or none of us will wake at dawn as we've got to do. I wait to make sure that he's really asleep. He might thrash and cry out, wanting someone who isn't there. His lips are parted and there is saliva shining at the corner of his mouth. The room smells of brandy and there are raindrops shining on the window. Richard lies in a swill of light from the lamp and it's like being in a pub on a rainy day, with the light wet and sexy and the whole of an afternoon's drinking ahead. Sweet and useless.

I was dead to him in the garden but now I'm aching. It could have been a slow, perfect fuck, but I didn't give it my attention. I lean forward. It's a bad angle and I can't get the position I want. He feels me, and shifts and sighs, but he's beyond waking. He smells of brandy, of sour fear, of the café's grease smell which cooked into us for hours. I kneel by the sofa and put my lips over his. My Isabel. *Come on, Neen, why can't you ever keep up?* His lips are full and warm. I keep my eyes open and his pores and lines dissolve as I come close, into a new strange country. I press my lips on to his, and then release the pressure so his lips swell back into shape. Press and release, press and release. My mouth stops feeling like my mouth, the way your finger ends do when you put them together and push them in and out a few times. I lean down into him. After a while I don't know where I stop and he begins. I try to fit my mouth exactly on to his, nought to nought. He's awake. He must be. But he stays still, letting me do everything. I breathe into his mouth and imagine my breath spilling down the bright branches of his lungs, until it crosses into his blood. Under the heel of my hand his heart bumps slowly and steadily. He's not awake. I edge his lips all round with minute kisses, and then I walk away, my bare feet light on the boards.

I go upstairs, and pause outside Isabel's room. Very quietly, I move right up to the door and put my ear against it and listen.

There's nothing. No one waiting with that smile on her lips which I'm never going to get from anyone else. I say her name aloud, hearing it hollow and stupid in the house which she's shucked off. A floorboard creaks as my weight shifts. There is no one there. I'll come back.

I've got something to do first. I creep on down the corridor to the turn, and Susan's room.

Susan's asleep, too. A bar of light from the corridor cuts across the room and shows her blond head gone dark, burrowing under the duvet. She's turned away from the door, and away from the cot. The room is stifling with baby and female scents. Edward's mobile turns above the cot, in the draught from the open door, and the fish ride on the end of their invisible threads. Edward must have come in here and fixed it some time during the long evening when he and Susan waited for news. He's put a hook in the ceiling.

It's a small room, about twice the size of the boxroom over the stairs where Colin slept in our house in St Ives. The baby is asleep under his cotton blanket, sleeping on his side with his round cheek pressed against the sheet. Slowly, silently, I let myself down until I am kneeling beside him, looking at him through the bars of the cot.

There was a poem my father loved, which he would say to us before we went to sleep. He would walk over to the window and look out at the bay, and the Island, and the darkening sea. He was ready to go for a drink as soon as we were in bed, and we'd hear the half-crowns chink in his pocket. But he'd stay for a while, walking around our room and saying the poem.

My mother wore a yellow dress,
Gently, gently, gentleness.

Come back early or never come.

My mother never wore a yellow dress. She wore overalls that smelled of clay and dust and she worked all day long and earned more money than my father. She had to. What he earned was less than he needed for drink. She was strong. The poem went on and grew fierce and strange so I pushed up tight against warm Isabel:

> *The dark was talking to the dead;*
> *The lamp was dark beside my bed.*

> *Come back early or never come.*

My father had known the man who wrote the poem. They used to drink together in London, and once he got my father some work on the radio and we all listened.

'*Come back early or never come,*' my father repeated, one last time, after the poem was over, and his voice made the room shiver. Isabel sat up in bed. 'That's stupid,' she said scornfully, shaking back her hair. '*Come back early or never come.* Why does he keep saying it?' My father laughed. 'You've got the soul of a potato, Isabel,' he said, 'like other beautiful girls I can think of.' Isabel wasn't crushed, as I would have been. 'I don't like any of that poem, anyway,' she went on. 'It sounds slippery when you say it.' I knew what she meant. A poem like that slipped into you like a knife and made you feel things you didn't want to feel.

'You'd do better yourself no doubt,' said my father. There was still a smile in his voice but soon there wouldn't be.

'I would. I'd just say what I meant.' Isabel thumped down flat on the pillow again.

'It's never as easy as that,' said my father, 'as you'll find.'

'Suit yourself,' she said. It was a phrase of ours at the time, and he went out without kissing us.

The baby snuffles, his lips against his hands. It's her smell he's looking for but she'll never come, early or late. When he looks up there'll be no face or shadow, no perfume. Isabel's gone, and her absence will grow along with him, getting bigger every year. He could be lying in her arms now, sodden and bruised by stones, on a grey foreshore where the tide's taken her. She would have held him tight, locked her arms round him. Before she went away up the beach she asked Pat Newsome if she ought to take the baby with her. She called him Colin. She must have thought Colin had come back, using her body, feeding on her. No wonder she stopped breast-feeding him. When he'd learned to speak, what would he say?

I stand up, and lean down over the cot and the sleeping baby. Gently, so as not to wake or startle him, I put my hand against his face. I spread my fingers and feel the warm thread of his breath, like a feather tickling my palm. His face is so small. My hand covers it completely, blotting it out. At once he moves his head to the side to free his mouth and nostrils. Gently, lightly, my hand sinks down again. He moves again. He moves strongly, wriggling away from under my hand. My father was right, things are never as easy as you think. It must have been hard to do. Colin was older than Antony, and stronger. His legs must have drummed the mattress a long time. Maybe she was afraid halfway through, and took the pillow off and saw what he looked like and knew she couldn't go back now. She'd gone too far and it was already beyond undoing. She had to go on pressing harder and harder till the movement stopped and there was no more little mewing from under the pillow. By the time he went still she must have hated him for taking so long to be dead. And at the same time maybe she still wanted to go back, and told herself he'd be alive again in the morning.

'Nina! What are you doing?'

I turn and see Susan sitting up in bed. Her eyes peer at me, shrunken with sleep. 'What's the matter? Was he crying?'

'No, he's fine. I just came in to have a look at him.'

'Oh.' She's ill at ease, suspicious, dragged out of sleep and wondering if I've come up to check on her.

'I'm sorry, Susan, I didn't mean to wake you up. I wanted to make sure he was all right. He's all I've got left of her.'

It works, as I knew it would. 'Oh, Nina, I'm so sorry. It must be terrible for you. Everyone thinks about Richard, but she was your sister. You'd known each other all your lives. Do you want to pick him up? I don't suppose he'd wake.'

'No.'

I stroke the side of the baby's face with my finger. Now he's rolled on his back I can see for the first time that he's not going to look so very like Colin after all. There's a lot of Richard in him too. I slide my finger across his open palm and he grasps it tightly, as if he knows me.

'It's all right, Ant, I'll look after you,' I tell him in a whisper, but he's asleep and anyway he knows it already. The whole world's here to look after him. He'll be a big, heavy man, like his father, a good man who believes the best of the world until it shows him otherwise. He's not going to grow up with words haunting the corner of his room. He's going to grow up with Isabel's shadow gentle on him. I'll say nothing. Nothing.

Chapter Thirty-one

I take down Isabel's key from the lintel again, open the door, put on the light. Edward didn't draw the curtains so there's an edgy sense of being watched by the black, reflecting square of the window. But there's no one out there, so I fight the urge to pull the curtains across. Let the night look in if it wants to. The night where Isabel's gone. On her bed there's the mark where a body has lain. Edward. The covers were pulled tight earlier, the way she'd left them. The drift of papers, books, clothes and sewing that usually covers Isabel's bed has disappeared. Edward's long, light body has made a deep dent. He's been lying there with his face in Isabel's pillow, silent, the door locked against us. For him it's all over. He'll be down at the sea now, straining into the dark as we did until black and white dots spark at him and his eyes itch with tears. He'll keep believing he's seen something. But there's so much sea, and so little land.

Edward won't sleep. He stayed awake before, when Isabel needed him, when I heard their voices murmuring under her door, hour after hour. I thought they were picking over the bones of Edward and Alex, Alex and Edward, but now I'm not so sure. If only I could hear their voices now, and listen to what Isabel was telling him. What did Isabel tell him? He was always closer than I thought. Closer to what nobody else should have known.

Edward will stay awake for Isabel while Richard sleeps, breathing loudly through his mouth because of the brandy. Edward won't see anything and he won't hear anything, only the restless noise of the water. The sea sounds so much louder at night. It sucks and drags at the stones, and if you listen it'll suck the heart out of you too.

I'm not going to think of Edward or what Edward sees. It's too late for that now. I've got my point of view and he's got his and we've got nothing to say to each other. And he's lucky, because he's got nothing left to do, and nothing he should have done. He did what he could. Let him stand there, let the wind blow tears into his hair. He can mourn for Isabel and I can't.

One by one I open the drawers by Isabel's bed. The bottom drawer is full of letters, stuffed in anyhow. I'll come back to those. I'm sure they won't give anything away, or Isabel wouldn't have kept them. There's half a packet of dried apricots in the second drawer. I slide the drawer in, and then pull it out again. The drawers are dark oak and they stick a bit, so you have to lift them a little as you slide them in. Finding food tucked away in the oak drawer reminds me of something.

We had a sideboard in this wood, an oak sideboard that should have been polished but never was. It was sticky with fingerprints. And there was a deep drawer in it. I touch the packet of apricots. They should be plump and moist but the packet's been open too long, and they are dry. I push them to the back of the drawer and my wrist scrapes on the inside wood. Yes. There was food kept in the deep drawer at home. There was an opened tin of Colin's milk, which no one knew about but me. My mother must have forgotten that she'd put it in there. There was dull blue paper on the side of the tin which I dug at with a fingernail while I scooped milk from inside with the little yellow scoop that was left on top of the heap of powder. The powder had a crust over it. I broke through it and ate the milk powder quickly, scoop after scoop, cramming it into my mouth. It was thick and sweet and disappointing. I knew it would taste better if I could make it up into a bottle the way I'd seen my mother do. Those bottles Colin grunted and flailed for. When he got them he sucked till sweat came out on his head and his baby smell was so rank it sickened me. I didn't dare take the tin out of the drawer. Isabel would have seen. The milk powder stuck on the roof of my mouth and in between my teeth so that long after I tiptoed away I could still suck on the taste.

There was torn paper over the top of the tin, like a circus hoop after a dog had jumped through it. I put the top back on the tin and hid it in the deep drawer. I went back to it again and again, not every day but when I could get away from Isabel, until the bottom of the tin shone through the last grains of the milk. After that I didn't go back.

I go through the contents of Isabel's drawers. An empty pill bottle, a red plastic file with details of antenatal care and maternity benefits. A catalogue from a rose nursery. An address book and her diary. We were always looking for each other's hidden diaries in our teens, but even when I found Isabel's there was never anything worth reading. This one is just the same. I flick through doctor's appointments, train times, neat notes: *E arriving. R in Hong-Kong, N b/day.* There's tomorrow's date, ringed in red, with *'Baby due today'* written in the space underneath, and then crossed out. When she was first pregnant the hospital got the date wrong.

If that first date had been right, Isabel would be alive. She'd still be pregnant, alive, slow-moving, sitting on the edge of her bed and pencilling in more dates, more *'things to do'*. But there's a quick, clean line through the date.

Her nightdress isn't hanging over the chair any more. I glance round but it's nowhere to be seen. Unless Edward's tidied it away, he's taken it. It's the old lace nightdress Isabel found in a second-hand shop and dyed. Isabel finds bargains everywhere, and she hardly ever needs to buy anything new. The lace at the neck was torn but she didn't bother to mend it. 'It looks OK as it is.' It did. It looked perfect. The soft, clear brown swell of her breasts against the torn coffee-coloured lace. But the trouble with being so beautiful is that people don't think you need anything.

The drawers are still open. I've looked at everything and

there's nothing left to find. But my hand slides in again, grazing on the wood, crackling against the thick layers of newspaper with which she's lined them. My hand moves of itself. Like a burrowing animal it feels deeper, lifting the newspaper, scratching the unstained wood beneath it. The wood is rough. My hand pushes back and back, deep into the drawer. I run my tongue over my palate, as if the clogging taste of milk is still there.

And I find Isabel's hiding-place. I draw it out, the piece of thin card that slips under my hand, glossed on one side. The photograph. It's face down, creased as if it's been crumpled up, and then spread flat again, for keeping. I turn it over.

It's a black-and-white photograph. A good photograph, sharp, clear and alive. It could have been taken yesterday. There is a woman, my mother, with the soft heap of a child in her arms. Its shawl trails down her dress, and one baby fist clutches a fold of wool. My mother is looking out at the photographer, lifting the baby up a little so that his face is clear of the shawl. She sits erect but easy, as my mother always sat. Her eyes look straight at me, proud, tender, triumphant. Look what I've done. Look what I've made. She offers me the baby so I can see how beautiful he is.

I draw in a long, shaky breath. It's my mother, but I don't know her. My mother, mine and Isabel's, never looked like that.

Isabel must have taken the photo, stolen it away. But she hadn't been able to bring herself to destroy it. She'd crushed it up, and then smoothed it out again and hidden it where she didn't have to look at it.

But I think she did look at it. When she was pregnant, when she was writing down her birth plan in the maternity file that no one's taken away yet. When Ant was born and she brought him home. She looked at the photograph again and again and she began to understand it. It was very simple, after all, when you came to look at it. Love, and hope. She saw them and she was afraid. I look round and for a second the empty room swarms with Isabel's terror, as my mother smiles in my hand.

It's easy to tear the photo. I tear it along the creases, then again, into pieces no one could ever recognize. I think of swallowing the pieces. I'm too tired, not thinking straight. Instead I put them in my pocket like confetti, and then I shut all the drawers. There's no point going through Isabel's letters. She won't have written anything down. All she's left is the photograph, but that's enough. She knew I would look in her drawers and find it.

But I don't know why she bothered to lock this room. There's nothing here for anyone else to find. When Colin died the smell of baby went out of the house at once. The next morning I clattered down the bare wooden treads of our stairs, and no one hissed at me to be quiet. There was no baby to be woken. I was the youngest person in the house again. Whatever Isabel has thought and felt here, it can't be found. I don't like words like soul and spirit, I never have. I walk around the room touching things: her hairbrush, her cool collection of marbles in its tall sweet jar, her books. The marbles have coils of colour in them which only come alive when they are spun across the floor. Some of them are chipped from fights. There are Richard's things too but I don't touch these. There's this to do first, before I can start to think of him. I pick up her comb and then put it down. It's grubby, with long brown hairs twisted in the teeth. She'd have combed her hair before she went out.

I loved this room when it was empty, just after Isabel took on the lease of the house. It seemed an enormous thing to do. I came down for a week to help her paint the bare rooms. We slept in here, on two mattresses with sleeping bags, side by side. The whole house stank of paint and we kept the windows open all night though it was cold. The rooms looked huge at first, and then as we painted them they gradually grew smaller. We mixed colours ourselves: I can still see dark stripes under the paint by the light switch where we tried out blends that didn't quite work. Beyond the windows there was the jungle of garden, all bind-weed and feral cats. 'Isn't it beautiful?' Isabel kept saying as we walked from one room to another, making echoes, deciding on colours, washing down walls and ceilings with sugar soap. She wore a pair of jeans which had been expensive once, a pair I'd always envied, but they were old now and she let them get covered in paint. One day it was sunny and we spent half the morning washing filth off the windows until we could see out of them. There was no hot water and no heating except for a couple of ancient electric fires that spat showers of sparks. It seemed like the most beautiful place in the world that weekend. I couldn't believe I'd ever want to be anywhere else, or with anyone else. But I went back to London, and Isabel met Richard.

I look around the room again, and now I know why Isabel locked the door. It was not to keep us out. It was to draw a line under the new life which had begun for her in that room, alone: she'd had the empty house around her with new paint on the walls like sunshine, and the lease in her own name, and she was miles from where we were born. For a long time she didn't bother to put up curtains at the windows. Everything was beginning.

I turn off the light and go to the window. There's a faint grey and I look up for the moon, but it's gone. The grey is dawn and it's not the day of Isabel's death any more. The more I look, the more I can see. Trees, lawn, Isabel's twisting paths, the garden wall. They jump into position like cats.

I always forget how much noise birds make in the country, how much they want each day to begin. The garden is soaked, but there's green spreading through the grey. There are low, dirty clouds over the water-meadows. No heat any more, no more blaze of summer. We're not cut off now and anybody can come here. Policemen and health visitors and neighbours with greedy eyes. Everyone will want to see the baby to make sure he's all right. I've been awake so long it feels as if I will fall to pieces unless I hold on to what I'm seeing for myself through my open, burning eyes.

Isabel's garden. From up here the shapes are clear. The paths run as she wanted them to run, secretly. You can lose yourself in this garden. There are the walls, dripping fruit, the flowers, smashed down by the storm. They are grey now, but in a few minutes colour will stain them. It's getting lighter all the time.

I remember the wilderness of weeds that was here when Isabel came to the house. She hacked and chopped and burnt until there was nothing left, and then she made her garden. But you never really get rid of nettle and ivy and ground elder and bindweed. As soon as you turn your back they spring up. The lines of Isabel's paths look like writing from up here, but it's writing that doesn't mean anything. She won't come again with her quick hands, digging and planting, ramming sticks into soft-ened earth to support the smashed flowers, making sense of everything.

It's first light, and the search will be resuming. Even as I watch, the sodden grass turns greener. I've never seen a police search but I know what they look like from years of TV. I'm stuffed with TV truths like everyone else. Lines of black, solid, tramping figures advance in a way that makes you want to run. They poke every foot of the earth with sticks, and mark it with tape. A search at sea is not so easy. A body won't lie where it's fallen. The sea plays with it, picking it up in its soft mouth, dropping it again. At the Gap the water's thick and green and you can't see to the bottom of it. I don't know what happens to people when they drown at the Gap. When they die and go down. But the searchers will know where's the best place for a body to be found. In broad daylight, with the storm over, the police will be able to look everywhere. Maybe she'll come up miles away and frighten children who are lying asleep in bed now. This is Isabel I'm talking about. My sister Isabel. Her skin is puffed and sodden, as it used to be when we stayed too long in the bath.

'Isabel,' I say, but the room doesn't answer and the garden keeps on growing, choking the paths with weeds, forcing through the brickwork. I think of how hard you have to work to make anything, and I feel tired.

Behind me there's a small cry, then another. The baby's waking up. But I stay, looking out of the window. Over the wall there are the water-meadows, flat and wet in morning light, and the hidden river that goes down to the sea. The baby is crying strongly now. The rising cry breaks on a second of silence, and I think it'll never come again. My palms prickle and I hold the window-sill as the house hangs still, suspended. But then the silence tears in a roar of outrage. He was only getting his breath.

I remember. I'm climbing up a long staircase cut into the rock, with my sister just in front of me. She's holding my hand, pulling me up until I'm safe beside her. I am four, and she is seven. I know she won't let go of me, though my face is sore with tears because she said if I didn't start climbing she was going to leave me behind. Sobs burst out of my chest like hiccups. Isabel looks back and down.

'There's only a few more steps. Don't cry, Neen.'

But I've got too much crying in me. 'You said you were going to leave me.'

She bends down and her cold fresh face almost touches mine. 'I'd never do that, Neen. You know I wouldn't. I'd do anything for you.'

Isabel's voice is stronger than the hungry sea under us. 'Would you? Would you really?' I stare up at Isabel, who could change the world for me. My mouth fills with the taste of milk. It clings to my tongue and sticks there. I smell milk, too, and the smell of baby, rank and sickening, blotting out the smell of the sea, blotting out everything. The baby is everywhere. It fills my ears and my mouth until I can't think of anything else. My lips move and Isabel bends to hear me.

'Will you really do what I want?'

'You know I will,' she answers.

Her eyes are so close to me I can see nothing else. I swim in their clear, wide blue. A huge, wonderful idea is unfolding in me like a clean handkerchief to wipe away all my tears.

'Isabel,' I say, 'when we get to the top, can I ask you something?'

She nods, her cheek brushing my lips. We go on up the endless staircase, hand in hand.

Visit Penguin on the Internet
and browse at your leisure

- ◆ preview sample extracts of our forthcoming books
- ◆ read about your favourite authors
- ◆ investigate over 10,000 titles
- ◆ enter one of our literary quizzes
- ◆ win some fantastic prizes in our competitions
- ◆ e-mail us with your comments and book reviews
- ◆ instantly order any Penguin book

and masses more!

'To be recommended without reservation ... a rich and rewarding on-line experience' – Internet Magazine

www.penguin.co.uk

READ MORE IN PENGUIN

In every corner of the world, on every subject under the sun, Penguin represents quality and variety – the very best in publishing today.

For complete information about books available from Penguin – including Puffins, Penguin Classics and Arkana – and how to order them, write to us at the appropriate address below. Please note that for copyright reasons the selection of books varies from country to country.

In the United Kingdom: Please write to *Dept. EP, Penguin Books Ltd, Bath Road, Harmondsworth, West Drayton, Middlesex UB7 0DA*

In the United States: Please write to *Consumer Sales, Penguin Putnam Inc., P.O. Box 12289 Dept. B, Newark, New Jersey 07101-5289*. VISA and MasterCard holders call 1-800-788-6262 to order Penguin titles

In Canada: Please write to *Penguin Books Canada Ltd, 10 Alcorn Avenue, Suite 300, Toronto, Ontario M4V 3B2*

In Australia: Please write to *Penguin Books Australia Ltd, P.O. Box 257, Ringwood, Victoria 3134*

In New Zealand: Please write to *Penguin Books (NZ) Ltd, Private Bag 102902, North Shore Mail Centre, Auckland 10*

In India: Please write to *Penguin Books India Pvt Ltd, 11 Community Centre, Panchsheel Park, New Delhi 110017*

In the Netherlands: Please write to *Penguin Books Netherlands bv, Postbus 3507, NL-1001 AH Amsterdam*

In Germany: Please write to *Penguin Books Deutschland GmbH, Metzlerstrasse 26, 60594 Frankfurt am Main*

In Spain: Please write to *Penguin Books S. A., Bravo Murillo 19, 1° B, 28015 Madrid*

In Italy: Please write to *Penguin Italia s.r.l., Via Benedetto Croce 2, 20094 Corsico, Milano*

In France: Please write to *Penguin France, Le Carré Wilson, 62 rue Benjamin Baillaud, 31500 Toulouse*

In Japan: Please write to *Penguin Books Japan Ltd, Kaneko Building, 2-3-25 Koraku, Bunkyo-Ku, Tokyo 112*

In South Africa: Please write to *Penguin Books South Africa (Pty) Ltd, Private Bag X14, Parkview, 2122 Johannesburg*

BY THE SAME AUTHOR

A Spell of Winter
Winner of the Orange Prize

Catherine and her brother, Rob, do not know why they have been abandoned by their parents. In the house of their grandfather, 'the man from nowhere', they make a passionate refuge for themselves against the terror of family secrets. 'An electrifying and original talent' *Guardian*

Zennor in Darkness

As U-boats nose the Cornish coastline, the village of Zennor is alive with talk of spies. It is a world of secrets and suspicion, and no one is immune. Not Clare Coyne, nor her beloved cousin John William, who is home on leave from the trenches, shell-shocked. Not D. H. Lawrence and his German wife Frieda, who have retreated from London to a cottage in Zennor ...

Burning Bright

Runaway Nadine is set up by Kai, her Finnish lover, in a decaying Georgian house occupied by Enid, an elderly tenant, whose own love affair many years ago ended in violence. 'Be careful,' warns Enid. When Nadine discovers that Kai intends to rent her out to a cabinet minister with special tastes, the warning assumes a prophetic quality. 'One goes on addressing the problems of evil which Dunmore raises long after one has finished her electrifying book' *Sunday Times*

Her collection of short stories:

Love of Fat Men

'Helen Dunmore is one of the brightest talents around and these stories show the full scope of her talent ... Exquisite writing adorns every page, marvellous flashes of poetic insight' *Sunday Telegraph.* 'Dunmore's new collection of short stories ... have the crisp delicacy of a snowflake and a snowflake's unexpectedly piercing sting' *Sunday Times*